Across the Second Dead Line

J.L. Fredrick

More Novels by J.L. Fredrick

The Gaslight Knights
Thunder in the Night
The Great Train Robbery of Monroe County
Mad City Bust
September Ten
Aftermath
Cursed by the Wind
Another Shade of Gray
Across the Dead Line
The Other End of the Tunnel

Non-Fiction
Rivers, Roads, and Rails

For Jan, Jill, Kari, Eric, and Lars.

Across the Second Dead Line

This is the story of three boys. Actually, they are young men, but because they haven't really entered—officially—into the adult world when the story begins, let's allow them to be called boys. You'll meet them face-to-face on the pages immediately following.

In every town there always seems to be those charismatic characters that everyone wants to embrace, yet, feeling intimidated by attractive looks, superior intelligence, or extraordinary abilities, no one does.

Robby Gladstone, Grant Kraemer, and Keith Bradley are three such characters; handsome, smart, rich, athletic, enthusiastic, rich, talented, energetic, rich, trustworthy, and did I mention rich? Yes, they happened to be three of the most fortunate kids on the planet, sired from well-to-do parents who love them and provide for their very comfortable lifestyles. But please don't look upon these three boys as spoiled brats, snobs, or any other derogatory adjectives that might come to mind. Yes, their fathers are all wealthy professionals, but they are not snobs, either. They are hard-working and responsible citizens who have simply considered life as not a matter of waiting out the storm, but rather, learning how to dance in the rain. For at least twenty years, they have been next-door neighbors in a town big enough to have storm sewers, but small enough for its residents to take pride in a traffic jam; a town where

they can be proud of their wealth, but where there is no
need to flaunt it publicly.

Their three sons who have literally grown up together,
so close that they could be considered brothers, have
earned a high level of respect and admiration from family
and friends. Through good times and bad, they have been
there for each other, ready to defend against foe; willing to
share any burden; able to comfort any sorrow.

But their bond is about to be broken; they are spending
their last summer together before they will each go off to
different prestigious colleges, so they might pursue their
dreams that have not yet been dreamt. Yes, their fathers
will pay the way, but only because the boys have already
proven their worthiness. It has been made quite clear that
the boys should not have to spend their last summer
together working at menial jobs that would make little or
no impact on their financial status entering college. The
final word: Let them be kids for one last glorious summer!

There comes a time in every rightly constructed boy's life when he has a raging desire to go somewhere and dig for hidden treasure.

Mark Twain

ONE

"You're crazy! That was a hundred years ago!"

"But there's still—"

"Keith is right, Robby. A hundred years is a long time. The place probably isn't even there anymore."

"And besides... if there was ever anything out there, someone would've found it by now."

Robby Gladstone wasn't willing to give up so easily. "Grant... Keith..." he said to his two best friends with the most sincere expression he could muster. "We've been best friends for as long

5

as I can remember, but I *can't* remember either of you ever backing away from something this exciting."

Keith and Grant exchanged glances. Robby had a good point; the three of them had played together in their adjoining back yards since they were toddlers, and they had remained best buddies all through their school years, played football and basketball on the school teams together, played in the school band together, hiked and fished and camped together, sang in the church choir together, and found their fair share of mischief together. Their families had become such close friends, they all spent Christmases and Thanksgivings together. Now, at age 18 or close to it, the boys' alliance still remained as strong as ever.

"So what makes you think it's so exciting?" Grant asked. The thought crossed his mind to at least listen to Robby's proposition.

Robby sensed that Grant was giving in a little. "'Cause according to these old journals, the one building that was left after the town burned down was haunted."

"Yeah, right," Keith said with plenty of sarcasm. "You really believe that?"

"I don't know... well, sort of," Robby replied. "You need to read these old journals I found in a box of Grandpa Vic's stuff up in the attic."

"He was the newspaper editor, right?" Grant said.

Robby nodded. "Yeah, and some college kid worked for him part time at the newspaper office back in the sixties... wasn't from around here... and he had some pretty wild experiences out there. He wrote all about it in his journal and he even wrote a book about it for a college class... got him and a friend of his in a lot of trouble, though, 'cause they discovered that many years earlier one of their college professors had committed a murder that was never solved."

"So, what happened?" Keith asked. Now he, too, was drawn in with a little curiosity.

"Well, you can read it all for yourself, but the professor was

6

ACROSS THE SECOND DEAD LINE

killed in a car accident before anything more could be investigated, and just before that happened Cory's friend, Buck was shot and wound up in the hospital—"

"Whoa, whoa, whoa," Grant interrupted. "Cory? Buck? Who are they?"

"Cory Brockway was the kid who worked for Grandpa Vic at the newspaper office and Buck Paxton was his college buddy... roommates in an off-campus apartment. Turns out that their land-lady was the daughter of the man who owned the old hotel at Silver Spring."

"The one *haunted* building that was left?"

"Yup. It was from that very building that Cory claimed—in his journal—that he heard piano music and voices... and even the sound of gunshots, but when he went inside, there was nobody there. Just a dusty, trashed old building. But there *was* an old piano."

"So how did your grandpa get Cory's journal?"

"It's not the original," Robby explained. "He made photocopies of all the pages one night when Cory accidently left it behind at the office during the trial. I don't think Cory knew he did it."

"Trial? What trial?"

"Of the guy who shot Buck. His name was Milton Sinclair. Cory says in his journal that Sinclair was even a friend of his and Buck's. He went to jail, but Grandpa always said he wasn't guilty; that he was set up. The cops had a lot of evidence against him, but he couldn't come up with a good alibi. They plea bargained and he went to jail for reckless use of a firearm."

"What's this?" Keith asked. He was holding a large brown envelope marked: *Evidence, Exhibit 22A.* He slid a leather-covered book out of the envelope.

Robby flinched. "Be careful with that! It's very old and a little fragile."

Keith altered his firm grip to a rose petal gentle grasp. "So... what is it?"

7

"It's another journal written by Clancy Crane. He was the hotel owner's youngest brother."

"How did your grandpa get it?"

"It was originally given to Cory Brockway by his landlady... seems she had possession of his last remaining personal belongings after he was killed in World War One. Somehow it ended up as court-room evidence in the trial, and somehow it was returned to Grandpa Vic about a year or so later. I don't know why... other than the note I found with it that Grandpa wrote... said the Sheriff thought it would make some good newspaper stories."

Keith carefully opened the cover and then flipped through some of the pages, lingering occasionally to sample some of the hand-written entries. "Wow. This is fantastic. Grant... come and look at this."

Grant was already busy scanning over the copies of Cory Brockway's journal pages. He laid them down on the end of the coffee table and shifted sideways on the couch next to Keith. Together they began reading as Keith gingerly turned each page.

Robby sat in an armchair facing them from across the coffee table. Silently his lips curled up in a grin, pleased that Grant Kraemer and Keith Bradley appeared to be mildly fascinated with the old documents. He sincerely hoped that he could convince them both to accompany him on an expedition out into an area that all local people simply called the 'Wilderness,' a territory where no one ever went.

"What are you boys doing?" a voice sliced into his concentration. Phyllis Gladstone, Robby's mother, came into the living room. He didn't think she was at home—she was supposed to be shopping.

"Oh... hi, Mom," Robby responded. "I thought you were at the mall."

"I was. Too many people there today," Phyllis sighed. "Hi, Grant. Hi, Punky." Keith had always been affectionately called *Punky* by the parents of all three families since he was a little kid, but now he was a *big* kid, and the three moms were the only ones still allowed to call him that—it was the unwritten rule. "You guys gonna have some lunch with me?" she asked. "I have some delicious shaved roast beef and sharp cheddar cheese for sandwiches and I just picked up a tub of mustard potato salad. Sound good?"

"Sounds great!" Grant replied.

"Sure... thanks!" Keith added.

After a long moment, Mrs. Gladstone hadn't heard a response from Robby. "How 'bout you, oh wondrous son of mine? Will you be joining us?"

"Yeah, sure Mom. Of course. I'm starved."

"Hey, weren't you supposed to mow the lawn today?" his mother said.

"Oh, yeah... I'll do it right after lunch."

Phyllis turned toward the kitchen. "Lunch will be ready in about fifteen minutes."

The three-boy choir sang out in unison: "Okay, Mom."

After a few more minutes of studying the old journal, Grant looked up at Robby. "You sure seem to know a lot about all this."

Robby stared a few moments at the kitchen door and then leaned over the coffee table, nearly whispering, guarding his voice carefully so his mother wouldn't hear. "I've read it over and over... many times," Robby replied. "Both journals and the book that Brockway wrote. Grandpa said in his note that this copy of the manuscript is not the same as the one Brockway turned in for the class. That one was sort of a fictional version of the real story... different names and the part about the 1937 murder left out."

"The *1937 murder*," Keith said, duplicating Robby's low voice. "You say that like there were more."

"There *were*... three that I can remember. First it was the stagecoach driver... I think his name was Dawson. He was killed during a holdup. Then Daniel Crane, and Jeremiah Crane, both of Clancy's brothers. Jeremiah was the hotel owner."

9

"What happened to them?"

"Daniel was about to be elected Town Marshall, and Dawson's killers were pretty sure that he knew they killed the stagecoach driver, and so before he became a lawman, they blew him away.

"Then it was a bank robber that came to Silver Spring expecting to meet up with his partner—his son, actually—and he and the hotel owner got into an argument, and the robber shot the hotel owner... killed him dead. And then he burned the town trying to escape the vigilantes who were hunting him down."

"Wow," Keith said. "This is quite a story."

"Well, there's a lot more to it, actually," Robby started to explain. "Towards the end of Cory's journal you'll read the part about him finding the loot from the bank heist in 1968. But the most interesting part that he *didn't put in the book he wrote* is the part about the *real treasure* that's probably still out there. It's all in his journal, though."

"So... what's the *real* treasure?" Grant whispered.

"Lunch is ready!" came the call from Phyllis in the kitchen.

"Take the journals with you and keep reading while I mow the grass... but don't let anything happen to them," Robby whispered. "We'll get together again tonight."

Two

When John Gladstone got home from work, Robby was still toiling in the yard with the *Lawn-Boy* humming in his hands. "Thought you'd be done by now," he said.

"Got a late start," Robby replied. "Just have that corner on the other side of the garden left."

John surveyed the yard's perimeter along the privacy fence. "I'll go in and change my clothes," he said. "And then I'll come out and help you with the trimming, okay?"

Robby nodded a thankful approval.

"What d'ya think about having the Bradleys and the Kraemers over for a barbeque this weekend?" John said as he loosened his tie. He was a diplomatic dad, and he nearly always involved Robby in making decisions like this. It would be the first big "family" get-together of the summer. The back yard barbeques were always wonderful—a good time and great food.

"That would be great!" Robby said as he pushed the *Lawn-Boy* to the un-mowed corner. A big smile suddenly occupied his face as it occurred to him that, although the boys had already had their own graduation party with the rest of their classmates, this would be the official "family" celebration, and a private family graduation party meant *graduation presents*! All the parents had been holding out, so this must be it!

While Phyllis Gladstone prepared a spaghetti supper that evening, she clutched the cordless phone between her cheek and shoulder, talking first to Judy Kraemer, Grant's mom, and then to Keith Bradley's mother, Karen. "Sunday's on for the cookout," she told them both, as if it had been tentatively planned in advance. She was acting very nonchalant as she discussed picnic food, but Robby was quite sure it was meant to be a surprise, although the boys had to be somewhat aware so they wouldn't go off somewhere, unable to be the guests of honor. Back yard cookouts were always the favorite way to celebrate birthdays and any other special occasions, weather permitting, except Keith—poor Keith—his birthday was in January. But there was always an extra cookout early every summer for no special reason other than to make up for it. But this wasn't it. Robby had it all figured out.

"Are you gonna have a cake for Keith's belated birthday this time?" he asked his mom, just as a test.

"Ahhhh... well... I guess we could do that," she said, as if she'd been backed into a corner. "Honey?" she called to John. "Should we order a cake for Keith?"

John strolled in from the living room. He started to say something, but then he saw Robby sitting at the table and immediately turned tomato red. "Sure... why not?" he said. "Supper about ready?"

"Go get washed up," Phyllis told Robby. "Supper's almost ready."

End of test, Robby thought as he headed to the bathroom. *They both performed just as expected.*

Later that night, in Keith's upstairs bedroom at the Bradley house, Robby felt obligated to inform Keith and Grant about his speculation on the up-coming barbeque. "Have either of you gotten a graduation present from your folks yet?"

"No," was the reply from both.

"They told me I had to wait," Grant pouted.

"Mine, too," Keith added.

"Well, I think the wait is over," Robby beamed. "The cookout on Sunday is supposed to be a surprise party for us... I think."

"Thought it would be my B-day B-B-Q," Keith said.

"Funny," said Grant. "I thought the same thing."

They practiced their *Oh-my-gosh-I'm-so-surprised* looks they would use on Sunday, but they were reluctant to speculate what their gifts might be. Each had been dropping subtle hints to the moms and dads about a car: *"Sure would be nice if I had a car so I don't have to bother you to take me somewhere,"* seemed to be the most frequently used; and, *"Sure will be tough at college without wheels"* was heard a lot, too. But it was bad luck to talk about it now—no need to jinx themselves.

THREE

A mid-June Sunday in Wellington couldn't have been more perfect for a cookout—clear sky, 75 with just a hint of a breeze. The Gladstone lawn was perfect, too; the grass a plush, smooth carpet of green and the fresh scent of roses and lilacs drifting through the air. Robby hoped someone would notice the effort he had put into its perfection. He'd spent nearly half his Saturday grooming, trimming, raking, and pulling weeds from the flower beds. Even if no one else noticed, it was still worth it—it always scored lots of points with Mom, and it usually netted him an extra twenty bucks in his allowance from Dad.

By eleven o'clock, Judy Kraemer and Karen Bradley were carrying bowls of baked beans, potato salad, *Jell-O* of various colors, and other picnic goodies across the back lawns. Two extra picnic tables came from the neighbors' yards to accommodate all the food and to make enough room for everyone to eat. It was going to be a grand feast.

Robby had changed out of his new blue jeans and white golf shirt that he wore to church that morning into a bright blue and white flowery Hawaiian sport shirt and white shorts. His mother had kicked him out of the kitchen so she and the other moms could efficiently get everything ready. He strolled out across the patio where his dad was about to light the charcoal grill.

"Need any help with that?" he asked.

"I think I have it all under control," his dad said. "But thanks anyway." Looking up into the sky, he added, "This is going to be a magnificent day."

Just then Robby noticed Keith and his dad, Bill, coming from their back yard, and about the same time Grant and Earl Kraemer, and Grant's little brother, Kevin appeared at the gate in the privacy fence. Grant and Keith both wore brightly-colored

14

flowery Hawaiian shirts and white shorts. They winked and smiled, and everyone knew the boys must have planned this stunning show of gaudiness.

They had. It was their style.

While everyone waited for the charcoal to get just right for grilling, Grant, Robby, Keith and Kevin started tossing a football around the yard, but when little Kevin missed a catch and the wildly bouncing football nearly landed in the potato salad, Grant suggested that they retreat to the safer distance of the driveway for a little two-on-two basketball. He knew his little brother was more proficient with a *round* ball.

So far, no surprises.

John Gladstone spent most of his time at the charcoal grill with Earl and Bill beside him, each nursing a long-neck bottle of cold beer. Any other time during indoor social activities, a Martini or Old Fashioned would be the beverage of choice, but on a warm summer day in the back yard by the barbeque grill, an icy cold beer seemed more appropriate. Two or three seemed necessary. Four or five seemed mandatory.

They were of varied professions: Bill Bradley was the General Manager of Sunflower Bakery that supplied bread daily to more than five hundred grocery stores in three states; John Gladstone was an investment banker at First National; Earl Kraemer, an electrical engineer, had designed a complex control unit for the Space Shuttle fuel system. Despite the different walks of life, they had plenty in common: they owned adjoining lots in a picture post card neighborhood; they had terrific wives and families, each with a son, all born in the same year; they enjoyed the same sports; they enjoyed back yard cookouts. And they all had enough money to make life quite pleasant.

The Porter House steaks proved superb, and when no one could eat another bite, Earl Kraemer rose to his feet at the head of the table.

"I want to commend John for the magnificent job he did with those steaks..."

Everybody clapped and cheered, and John stood up and took a little theatrical bow.

Earl continued. "I also want to thank the ladies for all the other fine cuisine. It was wonderful."

All the men and boys applauded.

"And then I have to compliment Robby for providing us with such beautiful surroundings... I saw him out here yesterday working his butt off making this lawn perfect for us."

More applause and Robby turned a bright shade of something resembling strawberries.

"And now has come the time to keep these three lads, our graduated sons, from thinking we have forgotten about their special day, of their truly great accomplishments, that is, surviving four years of high school."

Everyone laughed.

"But seriously... they have all been National Honor Society members four years running, star athletes *and* star students, graduating with Top Honors... what more can I say? How could we possibly ask for more wonderful kids? So now, let's send them off to college in style."

Robby noticed his dad pull out his cell phone, punch in a number, and then a few seconds later return it to his pocket.

Earl saw it, too. "So," he went on. "Without further ado... Boys? Your chariots await!"

The timing was perfect. It was obvious, now, that John's exercise with the cell phone had been a signal; up the driveway and right into the back yard roared a new, dark blue Jeep Wrangler. The driver quickly got out and ran back to the driveway.

"Grant," Earl said. "Happy Graduation from your mom and me."

Then, a moment later, a shiny, jet black Pontiac Grand Prix glided up next to the Jeep. Again, the driver exited the car and scurried back to the driveway.

Bill Bradley and his wife, Karen stood up. "Punky," Bill said.

16

"And I promise this is the last time I call you that... Keith... it's all yours. You earned it. Congratulations."

Without any delay, a bright yellow Mustang convertible came off the driveway and onto the grass, stopped next to the Grand Prix. The driver again disappeared down the driveway.

"Robby," John Gladstone announced. "Drive it in good health and with good sense." He put his arm around Phyllis. "We love you."

Leave it to the Dads to out-do their show of stunning gaudiness, and to concoct such a spectacular presentation. Moms and Dads clapped and cheered, and little brother Kevin threw in a few good ear-splitting whistles.

The boys stood there in their stunning Hawaiian shirts, breathless, speechless, tears. Never in their wildest dreams did they expect this today. They thought they had been so cunning with one up on the parents, ready to display their practiced surprise expressions, but to their great astonishment, they *were truly surprised.*

Grant was the first to regain his composure. He bowed his head, and Robby, standing next to him, saw the broadest, most genuine smile he had ever seen on his friend.

"Now we don't have to walk out to Silver Spring," Grant said so softly that only Robby heard him.

Robby gave a curious glance, brushed away his tears and threw one arm around Grant's neck, and then his other arm around Keith's. Then he stepped over to his mom and dad and gave them each a hug.

Keith and Grant did the same with their parents.

With all the joyful crying and hugging done, the moms brought out the digital cameras, and at least a hundred pictures had to be taken of the grinning boys standing by their shiny new cars.

Yes, it was a magnificent day!

FOUR

Lifestyles seem to change considerably when four wheels are placed under a boy in his late teens. The first thing Moms notice is the increase in laundry, as an extra change of clothes is necessary when the boy gets all wet from washing his car every day. Dads notice that chores now take half the time they did before, because the boy has someplace to go.

For the boy, though, the driveway in front of the garage is no longer merely a basketball court; it has now transformed into the parking stall for his new-found freedom. His world is no longer restricted to the distance reachable on a bicycle; the boundaries are removed, and the possibilities are limitless. Of course, the list of errands that Moms can conceive is limitless, too. Robby was quite certain that he would become even more familiar with the aisles at the *Hy-Vee* grocery store, and Dad's white dress shirts had to be picked up at the dry cleaners, and *"Would you be a dear and run down to the drug store to pick up my prescription?"* Then it was to return some books to the library, and... and... and...

Robby didn't mind so much, though, because it gave him a little extra justified time behind the wheel of his sporty yellow Mustang, and naturally, the top was down most of the time.

The Jeep wasn't in the driveway next door and he hadn't seen Grant for a couple of days. He knew Earl and Judy Kraemer had left for a vacation, and Kevin had gone off to some summer camp. But Grant hadn't mentioned anything about going away.

Returning from the hardware store to get a couple of new mouse traps for his mom, Robby drove around the block to Keith's house. Even though their back yards connected, the Bradley house faced the next street, so Robby couldn't see their driveway without going there. Keith had his Grand Prix pulled onto the grass in the shade of a huge maple tree. Half the hood, right front fender and door were all chalky white with drying paste wax. Sweat rolled down Keith's tanned, shirtless torso, and his dishwater blond hair looked like he'd just stepped out of the shower. When he saw Robby pull into the driveway, he tossed the polishing rag on the hood of the Grand Prix, stooped down to pick up a T-shirt laying in the grass which he used to wipe the sweat from his face. "We can do the Mustang next," he said with a grin. "I'm almost done with mine."

That was Keith... always eager to help his friends with whatever needed doing. Quite physically fit, tan, and with that always-ready-to-spring-into-action look, he tried real hard to always maintain the "tough guy" appearance. During the summer, if he wore a shirt at all it was usually a white sleeveless T-shirt with faded blue jeans most of the time. His hair was never combed, and a heavy silver chain usually draped around his neck. But under the tough guy veneer, his best friends knew a tender, gentle and caring spirit that they had always loved and admired.

Robby had just washed his car that morning. A coat of paste wax had crossed his mind, but then Phyllis had insisted that he go to the hardware store right away. "Okay," he told Keith. "I'll run these mouse traps over to my house so Mom won't have a fit, and then I'll come back and help you finish." He reached over the side of the Mustang and retrieved the plastic bag from the back seat.

While he was at home, he put on an old T-shirt and cut-offs— no need to get his good ones all sweaty.

"Where's your car?" "Phyllis asked. "I didn't hear you come in the driveway."

"It's over at Keith's... we're gonna wax it."

Phyllis knew there wouldn't be much point in requesting any more favors the rest of the day. "Will you be home for supper?" she asked.

Robby looked at the clock. It was already after three. "Don't know... maybe I'll eat at Keith's." There was never a need for any of the boys to wait for an invitation to share a meal with any of the three families; that had always been a standing policy among them. None of the moms questioned it; if there was an extra boy around at mealtime, she just set another place at the table. Likewise, if one was missing, she didn't worry that he was going hungry.

The hood and half the front fender of Keith's car was left to polish off the chalky wax when Robby returned. He grabbed a clean towel from the pile and started buffing the hood. This was nothing new to him; he'd helped his dad wax his Lincoln Mark VIII many times.

"Do you know where Grant went?" Robby asked. "The Jeep hasn't been in the driveway for a couple of days."

"Yeah," Keith replied. "He went camping with a bunch of guys in the four-wheel-drive club. He was looking for you, but you were gone somewhere when he had to leave."

"Probably at the grocery store for my mom," Robby said. "Is that the crowd he's gonna hang out with now?" He suddenly felt abandoned, and for a moment his feelings were hurt.

"No, I don't think so," Keith said. "He just asked them to teach him about driving off-road... figured they were the best ones to learn from. They were going out on some trail ride camping trip somewhere, and they invited Grant to tag along. Maybe they were figuring on recruiting a new member."

"Oh... well I guess that's okay." Robby smiled like the losers on a game show who have just been sent home with a year's supply of *Pepto-Bismol*.

"I think he said he'd be home tomorrow," Keith added. And then, as he wiped the last of the wax from the fender, he stood back to admire the shiny black car. "There... mine's done. Now we can do the Mustang. Pull your car beside mine in the shade."

While they polished Robby's Mustang, Robby asked: "Did you read any more of the journals?"

"Yeah," Keith replied. "I've read most of that real old one, but Grant has the other one at his house."

They were just finishing the wax job when Karen Bradley called to them from the front porch. "Hey, guys... dinner's ready." She had a place set at the table for Robby.

FIVE

"**Are you gonna get up** sometime today? Or are you waiting 'til Santa Claus has been here? It's only June, ya know."

Robby slowly opened his eyes. Grant's green eyes peered down at him from a towering distance. "It's a good thing you're not ugly," Robby mumbled. "I'd hate to wake up looking at something that big if it was ugly." Then he rolled over and closed his eyes again.

"It's eight-thirty," Grant said. "Your mom wants you to run to *Hy-Vee.*"

"Keys are on my dresser," Robby moaned. "*You* go to *Hy-Vee.*"

Grant grabbed a bare ankle that stuck out from under the sheet covering most of Robby; without any warning he drug Robby out of his bed. Robby sat on the carpet Indian style, rubbing his eyes. "Jeez," he whined. "Could you be a little more gentle next time?"

Grant just stood there laughing at his friend on the floor in his boxers. "Do I hafta drag you into the shower, too?"

Grant had a 13-year-old brother, Kevin, but he had always been big brother to Robby, too. Older by only two months, he stood six feet tall, a head above Robby. His height served him well on the basketball court; during his senior year he'd attained a 21-point game average playing point guard for the Wellington Wildcats. But just like Keith, who had caught four touch-down passes in the end zone for winning scores during his last year of high school football, neither of them were so outstanding as to achieve sports scholarships from any college.

Robby tried hard; he had been on both teams, but he warmed the bench most of the time, getting a little fourth quarter action when the coach was confident of a certain win. But his lesser athletic ability never affected the close camaraderie with Grant and Keith. To them he was just like any other teammate, and off the field or court, in their eyes, they were all equals. And best friends. It had been that way since pre-school. It would always be that way.

Phyllis Gladstone had breakfast waiting for both of them when Robby got out of the shower. It didn't matter that there was no one else home at Grant's house—he would've eaten breakfast with Robby anyway.

"I'm going to a Women's Club luncheon today," Phyllis said to Robby. "Would you please go and pick up some cottage cheese for me? I need it for the fruit salad, and I don't have time to go... oh... and while you're at Hy-Vee, get a dozen eggs, too... and a gallon of milk."

"Jeez, Mom... why don't you make a list?"

Phyllis shot him a look with daggers sticking out of it.

"I'll help him remember, Mrs. G," Grant said. "It's pretty early in the morning for Robby to be thinking straight, ya know."

Riding down the street in the topless Mustang, Robby asked: "So, how was the camping trip with the four-wheelers?"

"Oh, it was great," Grant replied. "I came over to see if you wanted to come along, but you were off somewhere, and they were waiting for me... so I had to leave right away."

"Yeah, Keith told me. So, where did you go?"

"About twenty miles on the other side of Red Hawk... one of the guys in the club has an uncle who owns about seven hundred acres of hunting land... hills, woods, a couple of creeks, and even a little lake. That's where we camped."

"Sounds like fun."

"It was."

"So, I s'pose you're gonna start hangin' out with them now, huh?"

"They asked me to join their club."

"Are you gonna?"

"I might go with them sometime on another trail ride, but I

23

don't think I'm ever gonna be a card carrying member."

"Why not?"

"They're not exactly my kind of friends."

"So, why did you go with 'em in the first place?"

"For a lesson in off-road driving... and they taught me a lot. Now I'll be able to get us out to Silver Spring."

Robby was stopped at an intersection. His head snapped around to look at Grant. "You really want to go out there?"

"Yeah, I wanna go out there. I think I know right where the dirt road is that Brockway wrote about in his journal. It takes off from Highway Forty-three about three miles out of town."

Robby was surprised—but pleased—that Grant had taken that much interest in Cory Brockway's journal. It made him forget about Grant abandoning him and Keith for three days. "So, you've read all of it?"

"Yeah... some of it three or four times."

"Think we'll be able to find the place?" Robby asked, and then the driver of the car behind them started honking his horn. Red-faced, Robby realized he was holding up traffic where there wasn't a stop sign; the Mustang's tires squealed a little when he took off. He sped down the street and turned into the back entrance of the Hy-Vee parking lot, hoping that the tan Impala wouldn't follow him in. It didn't.

"So, do you think we can find it?" Robby asked again when he parked in a space far away from all the other cars in the lot.

"Sure," Grant said. "He said it was about five miles off the highway, and he went over the tops of five ridges getting there."

"And he had to cross a stream—Silver Creek," Robby added.

"Yeah, I think we can find it... easy," Grant said.

"Think we'll get Keith to go?"

"If we don't let him read too much of Brockway's journal. He might freak out if he reads the part about Mack."

"You mean... the *evil ghost* that everyone back then believed was out there?"

"Yeah, and for all we know, he might still be."

"Oh, come on, Grant. Give me a break."

"Nobody ever proved that he *wasn't* there. And why do you think that we've *never* heard of anyone in our entire lifetime going out there to Silver Spring?"

"I don't know... but I'm sure everyone has forgotten about it by now."

"Don't be so sure," Grant said. "When I asked the four-wheeler guys if they had ever gone on a trail ride out there, they shunned me like I had contracted some weird contagious disease. They wouldn't even talk about it. So I don't think *everyone* has forgotten."

"Grant... do you really believe that there's some ghost out there guarding a treasure? A treasure that no one knows about?"

Grant glanced at Robby and grinned. "Do you really believe there *isn't?*"

"Okay. Let's go in and get this stuff for Mom... milk, eggs, and..." Robby stared at Grant for a long moment with a blank expression.

"Cottage cheese," Grant reminded him.

SIX

Keith had retrieved the basketball out of the Gladstone garage and was shooting hoops when Robby and Grant got there. "Hey," he said just as the ball swished through the net. "Mrs. G said you guys went to the store for her."

"Yeah," Robby said. "She's going to some Women's Club thing, and needed cottage cheese for the fruit salad."

"I know," Keith replied. "My mom's going, too. Guess we're on our own for lunch today."

"Well, we can go downtown to Abbey's for lunch," Grant suggested. "I haven't eaten there in a long time."

"I have," Robby said. "Burgers are great."

"I saw your Jeep," Keith said to Grant. "It's awful dirty."

"Yeah, it needs a good cleaning after that trail ride."

"Well, then, let's do it," Keith said. "And we can wax it, too."

By noon, they had the three cleanest, shiniest cars in all of Wellington. It was a hard decision which one to drive downtown for lunch; the black Grand Prix won the honors.

Abbey's Café had become an institution of downtown Wellington—one of the oldest establishments left. Most of the old, original downtown businesses had moved over the years to outlying strip malls and complexes nearer to the main highways that now bypassed the aging, historic business district. But Abbey's, now under management by the fourth generation of the same family, occupied a grand old brick building on the corner of Main and Johnson Streets. The exterior had been restored to its original Nineteenth Century appearance, and the interior replicated that era in a more modern, elegant fashion. One original fixture remained, though: a huge old *Regulator* clock mounted on the wall still ticked off each second that passed, just as it had done for over a century. Utilizing secret family recipes, handed down for generations, Abbey's Café was one of those unique restaurants that had remained a favorite dining spot for the locals, as well as travelers for longer than anyone could remember.

Abbey's Café was a busy place at lunchtime. Although the boys suspected that they should've delayed their arrival until after the noon rush, they had worked up quite an appetite cleaning and polishing Grant's Jeep. Just the thought of the tantalizing burgers, however, was worth the wait for a table. But the wait wasn't too long; a vacationing family had coaxed one of the waitresses to snap a photo of them at their table under the big, old clock. That

27

accomplished, the family left, the table was cleared and the boys were seated. They all ordered the infamous Ranch Burger and seasoned Curly Fries.

Robby plopped the folder containing the copy of Cory Brockway's journal on the table; he'd carried it in but kept it out of sight until the waitress had taken their order. Mostly strangers sat at all the tables around them, so he thought it seemed reasonably safe to talk about his proposed treasure hunt. He opened the folder and turned to one of the pages he had flagged. It was the entry that Cory Brockway described his third trip to Silver Spring in his *Ford Bronco*. "Grant, you know all about four-wheel-drive vehicles," he said. "Anything special about a Ford Bronco? Any reason it would be better than your Jeep?"

"I wasn't sure about that either," Grant said. "So I looked it up on the internet... to see what a Bronco back then was like. I'll guarantee you... my Jeep will go places where a sixty-six Bronco couldn't. Unless there's been an earthquake and the terrain has changed, we won't have any trouble getting there."

"I don't think there's been any earthquakes," Robby laughed.

Keith's big brown eyes widened. "You're going out there?" he said with enthusiastic anticipation.

"Yeah," Grant replied. "And you're going with us." He wasn't about to let Keith come up with any excuses for *not* going. They had always done everything together, and for one last summer before they would be separated by different college venues, it was going to stay that way.

"You didn't think I was gonna let you go without me, did you?" Keith said.

"Well, you didn't want to go four-wheeling and camping a few days ago."

"That was different... you were going with those *other* guys. It felt like the church choir going on a road trip with the Hell's Angels."

Grant chuckled. "Well, this'll be just us."

28

"Then I'm in."

"Of course, you're in," Robby said. Now there was a commitment; it didn't matter if Keith found out about Mack. He was going on this expedition, regardless.

"Now," Robby went on. "According to Cory's description of the trail, they were going west... or maybe a little southwest from Highway Forty-three."

"Does he say that? How do you know?" Keith asked.

Robby looked at Grant. "Wouldn't you agree? You've read all of this. They left Wellington early to mid-afternoon. Neither he nor Buck had remembered to bring sunglasses and he says they had the sun in their eyes when they weren't under the cover of trees. If the sun bothered them, then they must have been going west or southwest."

Grant nodded. "Yeah, I'd agree with that. And if they'd gone more south, they would've never come to the creek."

Keith wanted to know where they were talking about, because he had not been in on the earlier conversation.

"There's a dirt road that takes off from Highway Forty-three about three miles out of town," Grant explained.

"Oh, yeah," Keith said. "Dad and I went hunting out there once."

"How far out did you go?"

"To the end of the road... about two miles, I'd say."

"What did it look like after that?"

"Woods... but no more road."

"Well," Robby said. "Where that road ends is where our puzzle begins."

Just then the Ranch Burgers and Curly Fries arrived.

SEVEN

"Why didn't the four-wheeler guys want to go on a trail ride out to this place?" Keith asked after he had devoured half of his burger.

Robby and Grant exchanged glances. Grant nodded as if to tell Robby: *you tell him.*

"According to Cory's journal," Robby started, his voice low and guarded. "... a long time ago there was a legend about the place..."

"You mean Silver Spring? The town where Clancy Crane lived?" Keith asked. He had read Clancy's entire journal, so he was quite familiar with the town that no longer existed.

"Yeah," Robby replied. "The bank robbers... Zachary McDowell and Zach Junior—"

Keith interrupted. "They were bank robbers?"

"Yeah... well, when McDowell burned down the town after he'd killed Clancy's brother—"

"The hotel owner," Keith interrupted again. He wanted to make sure he was following the story correctly.

"Right..." Robby continued. "And Clancy jumped out from behind his brother's tombstone and clubbed Mc-Dowell and killed him... in revenge... somebody saw that happen, and probably because of all the smoke, someone started the rumor that it was Clancy's brother's ghost... risen from the grave."

"Yeah, I know that," Keith said. "Clancy told the hotel owner's wife later that he didn't want anyone to think differently... he was afraid he'd get in trouble for bonking McDowell on the head."

"Exactly. And then—"

"And then," Keith continued the story. "Clancy hid out in the woods until after everyone else had abandoned the burning town. He came back the next day, and then Zach Junior showed up... looking for his old man... that he didn't know was already dead."

"Sounds like you know the story pretty good," Robby said.

"But keep going," Grant chimed in. "I haven't read Clancy's version of what happened."

"Well," Keith continued. "When Zach Junior showed up, so did a bunch of looters—I guess they planned on ransacking what was left of the town—and then there was a gun battle, and some of the looters were killed. The survivors scrambled outa there... but there's one thing I don't understand."

"What's that?" Robby asked.

"Why did they think they had seen McDowell's ghost? That's what they told everybody."

"Okay... the reason you don't understand that is because you haven't read Cory's journal. He explains that very clearly: Zachary McDowell and Zach Junior looked very much alike—could've passed for twin brothers if one hadn't been older."

"Well," Keith said in deep thought. "How did Cory know that? Clancy never wrote that in his journal."

"No, but in 1967, Cory's buddy found a book at the public library while he was researching for a history project... it had a picture of the two of them, and if it hadn't been for that book, they would've never known that McDowell and his son were bank robbers."

"Oh, I get it now... the looters must've known that old man McDowell was dead."

"Right. They had seen Zach Junior, but they had everybody believing that Silver Spring—or what was left of it—was haunted by the ghost of McDowell Senior. They named him 'Mack.' When Cory Brockway was writing this journal in 1968, there were still a lot of people who believed it, and apparently, there are still believers today."

"So that's why the four-wheelers don't go out there?" Keith said. "Because they think it's haunted?"

Grant nodded and chewed the last of his curly fries. "Did your grandfather ever talk much about it?" he asked Robby. "And what about your dad? He must've been around then."

The Kraemers and the Bradleys had been newcomers to Wellington just a couple of years before Grant and Keith were born, however, the Gladstone family had lived in Wellington since Victor Gladstone, Robby's grand-father, came there in the late 1940s to become the editor of the local newspaper. If any of the three should have known about the Silver Spring legend, it would be Robby.

"Grandpa Vic talked about it some," Robby said. "Dad was seventeen in 1967, but he's never talked about it at all."

"Should we ask him?"

"I don't think so. Then he's gonna start asking questions, and I'm gonna get in trouble for digging in Grandpa Vic's stuff."

"So what's the big deal?" Keith asked. "We're gonna find a place called Silver Spring that everybody used to think was haunted." He said it loud enough for others around them to hear. Robby could feel all the eyes in the room staring at their table. He casually glanced around, trying not to draw any more attention; a few heads had turned. He looked back to Keith. "Shhhhh," he cautioned his friend discretely.

Grant realized, too, that they were being scrutinized by many of the other frowning diners. "Everybody done eating?" he said. "Let's get outa here."

EIGHT

This was the first time they had all been cruising together in Keith's Grand Prix. Quiet, air conditioned, and quite comfortable, it offered certain advantages over the open-air, top down Mustang or Jeep. They enjoyed those cars, too, but the Grand Prix was quickly becoming their cruiser of choice. Grant stretched out across the rear seat and sucked in the aroma of the new leather upholstery. Robby settled into the front passenger seat and soaked up the air conditioning. Keith grinned.

"So, tell me," Keith said. "What's the big deal about Silver Spring? Why were you being so quiet about it?"

Robby adjusted the position of his shoulder harness so he could face Keith and Grant. "Because... Silver Spring is apparently still a touchy subject for a lot of people... especially the older people who still remember what happened out there."

"Well, what exactly *did* happen out there that's got everybody so scared of the place?"

Robby took a deep breath. "It's probably more superstition than anything... Cory spelled out quite plainly that Professor Barkley had committed the murder in 1937, but because he was killed in a car crash in 1968, the cops kinda brushed it under a rug; the public never heard about it, and everyone still thought that a ghost named Mack was responsible."

"Murder? Who got murdered?"

"Some guy who went out there hunting for the treasure in 1937."

Keith squinted, straining to draw all the facts together. "But it was the college professor? What was he doing out there?"

"Looking for the treasure, too," Robby said. "But he had some inside information."

"Like what?"

"At first, everyone assumed that the *treasure* was a fortune left behind by the hotel owner, Jeremiah Crane, but that never really existed, and no one even knew about the bank loot. But then it turns out that Zachary McDowell was the professor's grandfather; Zach Junior, the professor's uncle, got caught and went to prison for the bank heist, and somehow the professor found out from him that the bank money was hidden at Silver Spring."

"But I thought you said *Cory* found the bank money in 1968."

"He did. Barkley never found it, but when this other guy showed up, Barkley whacked him with a shovel and killed him... buried him out in the woods. Of course, when the guy turned up missing, no one went looking for him, and Barkley was never suspected as the murderer. Mack was blamed."

"Oh, now you're giving me a headache," Keith moaned. "So, if Cory found the bank money, how much did he get?"

"Three thousand dollars."

"What'd he do with it?"

"Cory was already back in Florida when he called Grandpa Vic and told him about it. Grandpa Vic convinced him to just keep quiet about it. It had been so long since the money was stolen— like, seventy years—that it wouldn't make any difference."

Grant leaned forward from the back seat. "I don't remember any of that in his journal."

"Because the part about Cory calling him from Florida isn't in the journal," Robby explained. "Grandpa Vic told me that himself."

Keith pulled the Grand Prix into a parking space by the lake. "Let me get this straight," he said. "If Cory found the bank loot that no one else knew about and the hotel owner's fortune never existed, what are we going out there for? I thought you said this was a treasure hunt."

"It is," Robby replied.

"Let him read Cory's journal," Grant suggested. "And I want to read Clancy's. Then we'll both understand a little better."

NINE

Sitting at home alone in a quiet and empty house, Grant Kraemer found himself intrigued by the old, leather-bound journal written by Clancy Crane a century ago. It was just as Cory Brockway had described it in 1967: *Simply a letter that had been lost in the mail.* The penmanship elementary, spelling not always accurate, and grammar less than perfect, Clancy's words *did indeed* sing with a voice of certain eloquence that seemed to bring him back to life. Reading this journal, it was easy to understand how Cory Brockway, the college student in 1967, had been able to piece together so many accurate details about a place that was no more than a distant memory to just a few. Scattered throughout his entries, Clancy had laid out the entire town in a verbal map, describing each business place and its location in minimal simple terms. Perhaps, no other source, anywhere, of such information existed. Grant recalled from Cory's 1967-68 journal comments about the difficulty in locating any information about Silver Spring. Cory had eventually uncovered the reason for that: the professor and his girlfriend/librarian accomplice had purposely removed and destroyed all that was readily available in an attempt to disguise the truth, and to cover up his involvement in the 1937 murder. By keeping the ghostly legend alive, the professor was assured of continued avoidance of Silver Spring by the public and law enforcement, and the discovery of the body he had buried there. It seemed a little scandalous, too, that the police had chosen to prevent the news media from exposing to the public the actual fate of the man who had mysteriously disappeared in 1937. Mack and the legend lived on.

But the murder and the ghostly legend weren't Grant

Kraemer's top priority. Nothing could change any of that, nor did it really matter anymore. He was interested, though, in finding the passages in Clancy Crane's journal that had been noticed by the 1967 college student, and cleverly linked to another treasure that had been totally undetected by everyone except Clancy Crane... and Cory Brockway. Grant hadn't been quite sure what Cory meant when he wrote in his journal that *he thought he had somehow established a spiritual connection with Clancy Crane,* but now the meaning was becoming more evident. The hints would have been easily missed without a little help.

Growing up in the 1890s in Silver Spring, Clancy Crane was befriended by a newspaper reporter who had encouraged him to record his thoughts and observations in a journal; he stated that in his very first entry, writing that 'Tom' had given him the book as a present. He then must have copied into the book all his previous entries he had written somewhere else, as it went all the way back to when, at age ten, he and his two brothers and their wives first arrived at Silver Spring in covered wagons from Ohio.

He had been in the habit of writing most of his entries early in the morning—sometimes before dawn—sitting on the front verandah of Tanglewood Lodge, the hotel that his brother owned. Clancy was an early riser, often the first customer at the farmer's market to obtain the best produce for the hotel's kitchen. It was during those very early hours when the rest of the town was still asleep that he captured his thoughts of the previous days, and fortunately, because of his early morning practice, he made some very important observations.

Cory Brockway had made some astute observations, as well. He and his college buddy had found an article in some old newspapers handed down to their landlady—perhaps the only copies in existence of *The Striker,* Silver Spring's own newspaper, as all had been lost when an arson's fire completely destroyed the town in 1899. The article was about a laborer at the silver ore smelter who was shot and killed by a lawman. Oliver Pratt was suspected of stealing three 70-pound bars of pure silver from the smelter before they had been counted and delivered to the banking house. Late one night while he was retrieving one of them from its temporary hiding spot in the woods, the lawman who had decided to watch him confronted him in the act. There ensued a gunfight; Pratt was killed, and the other two bars he was suspected of stealing were never recovered.

Cory Brockway took notice when Clancy referred to a fellow named Oliver who lived in one of the rooms over the Continental Billiard Parlor. On many occasions, Clancy noted that Oliver had passed on the opposite side of the street from Tanglewood where Clancy sat unnoticed in the dim light of a single lamp on the hotel's verandah. A burlap bag containing some heavy object was always slung over Oliver's shoulder as he marched quietly up the street—never on the board sidewalk where his footsteps would resound through the stillness of the early morning. Just five minutes later he would return, following the same path down Main Street, but the bag, then, always appeared much lighter. Cory wrote that he counted eleven such entries. Then he had compared Clancy's notes with the news article. All the trips that 'Oliver' made past Tanglewood occurred during the months just prior to the shoot-out between Pratt and the lawman. After the date of the newspaper story, 'Oliver' no longer passed by the hotel toting the heavily-laden burlap bag.

It may have been bold to assume that Oliver Pratt had carried off more than *three* bars of silver from the smelting furnace, or that Clancy's 'Oliver' was the same man. But it seemed a logical conclusion that Oliver Pratt had stashed at least eleven bars of silver, maybe more.

TEN

Grant was sitting at the breakfast bar eating a bowl of corn flakes with Clancy's journal lying open in front of him. He had been up until after midnight reading it the first time, and now he wanted to reread certain parts.

The phone jingled.

"Hello?"

"Hey, Grant... Mom knows your folks aren't home yet so she says you should come over for breakfast."

"I'm eating a bowl of corn flakes."

"Well, forget the corn flakes and come over... Mom's making waffles. Keith's already here."

"Waffles?"

"Yeah. And sausage, too."

"I'm not dressed yet."

"That'll take you two minutes. I'll tell her you're on the way."

Before Grant could say any more, Robby hung up. Waffles and sausage sounded much better than corn flakes; Grant dumped what was left in the bowl in the disposal and scurried to his bedroom to find some clothes.

"Robby didn't wake you up, did he?" Phyllis asked Grant as he sat down at the table.

"Oh, no," he replied. "I've been up for a while."

Mrs. Gladstone set a plate with a steaming, golden brown waffle in front of him. "How 'bout you, Punky? Ready for another one?"

"Sure," Keith said.

Robby was already pouring syrup on his second.

When they had their fill of waffles and sausage, Phyllis asked, "So, what are you boys up to today?"

"Um, our cars are pretty dirty," Keith stuttered. "I think we need to wash them."

"Didn't you just wash them yesterday?"

"Well, you know, Mrs. G... it's pretty dry and dusty these days, and you know how the dew can really mess up a dusty car that sits outside overnight."

Phyllis laughed. She knew better than to dis-agree with a teen-aged boy on logic like that. "Have you heard from your mom and dad?" she asked Grant.

"No," Grant replied. "But I'm sure they're having a wonderful time in Washington."

The boys sat at the table nervously making eye contact with each other; they knew what was on each other's minds.

"Breakfast was delicious," Keith said as they slid their chairs back from the table.

"Glad you enjoyed it," Phyllis said.

The three-boy choir sang out, *"Thanks Mom"* as they headed for the back door.

No one to eavesdrop at the Kraemer house, they decided to continue their discussion about the treasure hunt there. Keith retrieved the copy of Cory Brockway's journal from his bedroom and caught up to the others in the Kraemer back yard.

When they were settled into the den, Grant said to Robby, "Cory Brockway figured out that there were a bunch of silver bars hidden somewhere. Do you think he might've come back to find them?"

"No," Robby said. "Grandpa Vic picked him up at the airport

40

when he came back for the trial. He stayed at Grandpa Vic's house all the while he was here, and Grandpa Vic took him back to the airport. He would've known if Cory went out there. And he would've known if... well... Cory never came back here again."

"Do you think it's possible that Cory really made a spir-itual connection with Clancy Crane?"

"I don't know... I mean... I think it's possible. I got the same feeling when I first read Cory's journal, too... even before I read the part about him and Clancy."

"What do you mean?"

"That Cory's spirit was connecting with me somehow."

"*His spirit?*" Grant asked curiously. He, too, had noticed a strange tingle as he had read Cory's words.

"Yeah," Robby replied. "Didn't I tell you?"

"Tell us what?" Keith said.

"Grandpa Vic stayed in close contact with Cory. He told me that Cory was diagnosed with Leukemia a year after the trial. He died in 1980."

"Oh," was the only reply from Grant and Keith. Their expressions drooped, as if it had been a close personal friend that just died. After all, they *had* become well-acquainted with Cory through his journal.

"Did Cory's book ever get published?" Keith asked.

"I don't think so," Robby said. "I think Grandpa Vic would've told me."

"Probably good it wasn't," Grant said.

"Why?" Keith asked.

"'Cause every treasure hunter in the country would've been there already."

"Do we know for sure that *someone hasn't* found it?"

"Something like that would've made national news," Grant said.

"Besides," Robby added. "We're the only ones other than Grandpa Vic who have ever seen Cory's journal. No one but Oliver Pratt and Clancy Crane knew it was missing... until Cory figured it out. They never told anyone, and they're all dead."

"But *someone* must've known there was that much silver missing," Keith argued.

"Probably not," Robby said. "In those days, they had no way of knowing for sure exactly how much silver a   wagonload of ore would yield. The ore was dumped into the smelting furnace, and after the whole process was done, the molten silver was collected in big pots, and then it was poured into molds to form the bars. A clever employee could've snuck one out now and then."

"Without anyone else knowing?"

"Sure... if it was just a little at a time. My guess is that back then there wasn't much security... a place like that ran on trust. In the middle of the night or the wee hours of the morning, whoever was pouring the silver into the molds probably had opportunities to slip one out before the bars were counted and taken to a vault. Oliver Pratt was apparently successful with that... for a while."

"And you don't think he had any partners?"

"Oliver Pratt was a loner," Robby said. "You can tell by the way Clancy wrote about him... like, he lived alone in a single room over the pool hall, and he always drank alone at the saloons, and he never talked to other people. No, I don't think he had partners."

Just then the phone in the den started ringing. Grant picked up the receiver. "Hello?"

"Hi, Grant," Phyllis Gladstone answered.

"Oh, hi, Mrs. G."

"Could you please ask Robby to drive his filthy, dirty Mustang over to Hy-Vee?" she said with a little sarcasm thrown in. *"I need some things for baking... and I have a list."*

ELEVEN

The dot matrix created in the faint layer of dust by droplets of dew was just slightly more noticeable on Keith's black Grand Prix and Grant's Patriot Blue Jeep than it was on Robby's yellow Mustang. All three, though, considered it a violation of the *Bradley/ Gladstone/ Kraemer Clean Car Act* put into law just days before. When Robby returned from the grocery store run, Keith and Grant were rinsing the soap off of their cars in Grant's driveway. He raised the top and closed all the windows before he pulled into range of the garden hose behind the Jeep and Grand Prix. Just as he suspected, they sprayed him with the hose as he exited the Mustang.

Groceries delivered and all three cars washed and dried, they stood shirtless between the cars, gently leaning against the waxed fenders.

"Clancy didn't say that he knew where Oliver hid the silver," Keith said. "And I didn't see anything in Cory Brockway's journal last night that indicated *he* knew, either."

"Did your Grandpa ever say anything about it?" Grant asked.

"No," Robby replied. "I doubt that Cory knew; if he did, he wouldn't have told Grandpa... or anyone else. But I think we can figure it out."

"How?" Keith asked.

"Clancy said he always saw Oliver walking on the opposite side of the street from the hotel, and then five minutes later he returned. When we find the hotel, we should be able to figure out what direction to go. It can't be too far from there."

"He did describe the town quite well," Grant said.

"But if they're buried, we could be there forever—"

"It's not buried," Robby interrupted Keith.

"Robby's right," Grant said. "He wasn't gone long enough to bury it. He hid them somewhere easier and quicker... like in a building."

"But according to the journals, every building in the town except the hotel burned down," Keith said.

"Right. So at the time, the bars could've been covered up by a pile of ashes, and ashes get blown and washed away by the wind and rain. They could be laying right out in the open now."

"You could be right," Robby said. "But I don't think it'll be that easy."

"Well, we'll just have to go out there and take a look around. Wanna go four-wheelin' and camping this weekend?"

ACROSS THE SECOND DEAD LINE

TWELVE

They had been camping together many times, but it had always been in campgrounds or easily accessible places to where Moms and Dads could haul them and their gear in the family cars, drop them off, and pick them up again in a few days. This was the first time they would head into the wilderness, them and all their gear packed into one little Jeep. They would have to economize.

By late afternoon they had set up three different tents in Keith's back yard, finally deciding on Keith's medium-sized dome tent because the pack took up less space, yet it was roomy enough to accommodate Grant's King-size air mattress that was large enough to fit three sleeping bags.

"Planning on sleeping out in the back yard tonight?" Karen Bradley asked when she came out to investigate all the tent building she had seen going on during the afternoon.

"Oh... no," Keith responded. "We're goin' camping for a few days... just seeing which tent will work the best."

"You see, Mrs. B," Robby explained. "We're going in Grant's Jeep, and with the three of us, there isn't a lot of room for a lot of stuff, so we have to pick the best *one.*"

"I see. Well, you can come in for dinner anytime... it's almost ready," Karen said as she headed back into the house.

The three-boy choir sang out, "Thanks Mom."

Bill Bradley had just come home from a busy day at the office. "So how's that new Jeep working out?" he asked Grant while they waited for Karen to finish setting the table.

"It's great," Grant replied. "I went out on a trail ride with the four-wheel-drive club. They taught me a lot about off-road."

"Yes, I heard," Bill said. "Keith mentioned that you'd gone out with them... can't imagine you hangin' out with that bunch, though."

"Aw, they're not so bad... once you get to know 'em... and they've got some pretty nice trucks."

"Suppose we'll see that Jeep lookin' like one of those monsters pretty soon, huh?"

"No, I don't think so," Grant said. "But I would like to get some better tires. That'd help it a lot."

"Karen says you guys are going camping this weekend."

"Yeah... I'm gonna get us out into the boonies somewhere."

"Well, there's a lot of places around to do that. I hear it's really good out on the other side of Bear Lake."

"The four-wheelers were telling me that, too," Grant replied. "Maybe we'll give it a try."

Bear Lake was in the opposite direction of where the boys planned to be that weekend, but none of them disagreed with the idea. The suggestion had disencumbered them from the need to camouflage their secret mission to Silver Spring; the less anyone knew about their discovery, the better. For now, at least.

Karen Bradley suddenly remembered something important as she put the big bowl of Sloppy Joe barbeque on the table. "Punky! Don't forget that you have a dentist appointment on Tuesday."

"Yeah, Mom, I remember," Keith said. "We'll be back before then."

Robby had always enjoyed the restful sounds of a rainstorm in the morning—the soothing hiss of the rain on the roof and the rolling thunder were almost therapeutic to him. He loved napping through the afternoon squalls that popped up out of nowhere. When he awoke Thursday morning, though, it took only a few seconds for his foggy mind to catch on to the fact that this was not one of those comforting rainstorms. The thunder booms sounded like a B-52 attack and vibrated the house; the menacing gray overcast that enveloped the morning seemed to unravel at the seams and dumped sheets of water out of the sky. Visibility was nearly nonexistent—Robby could barely see his yellow Mustang down in the driveway. This certainly didn't look like a good day to start a camping trip.

He picked up his cell phone and punched in the Kraemer's number. It rang ten times and went to voice mail. Apparently Grant was sleeping right through the storm.

Karen Bradley answered, though, on the third ring.

"Hi, Mrs. B... this is Robby... is Keith up yet?"

"Yes, he is. He and Grant just finished breakfast. They're watching TV out in the living room... just a minute..."

Robby heard her call out, *"PUNKY! Robby's on the phone."*

Keith picked up. *"It's nine o'clock, Gladstone... about time you got your butt outa bed."*

"Thunder woke me up."

"Just a little rain... no worry. Grant stayed here last night... we've been up since before it started."

"Looks pretty bad out there."

"It's not the beginning of monsoon season," Keith joked. *"We're watching the weather channel... it's just a little low pressure pocket moving through."*

"How long's it supposed to last?"

"Forecast is better than it looks... supposed to clear up this afternoon... should be nice and sunny all weekend."

THIRTEEN

By Friday noon the only evidence of the previous day's downpour was the vivid green on all the lawns, and even the trees looked refreshed and happy. And, of course, the dust had settled and the breeze carried the scent of neighborhood flower gardens. Just as the weatherman had predicted, there didn't seem to be any lingering threats of a ruined weekend outing due to climatic temperaments. It would be a great day to start a treasure hunt.

After a cheeseburger and potato salad lunch on the Gladstone patio, the Jeep was loaded with tent, air mattress, sleeping bags, cooler, and the other essentials deemed necessary for a weekend wilderness trek. They had enough food for three days, so the moms were informed that Monday was their latest planned return. There was no ceremonial send-off—just the usual *"Have fun and be careful"* departure—the only difference this time being the boys providing their own transportation to the campsite. When the Jeep pulled out of the driveway, Phyllis Gladstone casually headed across the back yard to have coffee with Karen Bradley.

In that Jeep, though, three enthusiastic boys were boldly heading off on a not-so-usual camping trip. Somewhat fearful of the unknown, their eagerness for the daring adventure remained the driving force that kept pushing them forward. The ages-old legend of a murdering specter named Mack could not stop them now, and they were quite certain that they were the only living creatures on the planet who knew of a treasure that had been lost to time and superstition; a treasure that had been hidden on a remote hilltop for over a century just waiting for them to find.

"Got enough gas?" Robby asked as he double-checked to make sure his duffel bag with the journals inside was within reach.

"Filled up the tank just this morning," Grant replied. "Checked everything over like the four-wheelers showed me... we should be good to go."

He slowed down and turned the Jeep onto the dirt road.

"Are you sure this is the right road?" Keith asked from the rear seat.

"I checked it out the other day. There's only one other dirt road off this highway for ten miles... and that one just goes to a farmer's hay field."

Robby had another good reason that this was the right place. "Cory Brockway walked this route when he ran out of gas, remember? For the amount of time it took him, it couldn't have been farther out of town. This *has* to be the right road."

The Jeep purred along the dirt trail, the first two miles of which, after leaving the highway gave no challenge. It had been well-travelled by hunters; four-wheel-drive wasn't even necessary. But the road simply ended after it had passed through a stretch of forest and emerged into a clearing at the base of an incline that was well-populated with large trees. This is where Grant could flex his muscles a little. He had put his four-wheeler through the paces on the trail ride, and he felt quite confident that he could impress his two passengers with the Jeep's *and his* performance here.

"Is this where you were hunting with your dad?" Grant asked Keith. He stopped the Jeep at the edge of the clearing.

"Yeah," Keith said. "It hasn't changed at all since last year. Dad shot a buck about two hundred yards that way." He was pointing off to their left.

Robby got out of the Jeep and walked to the front, scanning the forested hillside. He took off on foot into the trees.

"What are you doing?" Grant called out to him.

"Looking for a trail," Robby called back.

A few minutes later, he emerged from the woods again. "There seems to be some evidence of a trail through the trees straight up that way," he told Grant pointing up the hill.

Grant looked around. "Well, that's definitely west," he said.

"Then let's go!" Robby said and got back in the passenger seat. "If we keep the sun in front of us, or just a little to our left, we should be headed in the right direction."

The mid-day sun, however, was still nearly overhead, and jostling through the forest where there was no road, they quickly discovered that it wasn't so easy to keep a straight heading into the west, dodging trees and coursing the terrain in such a way as to keep all four wheels on the ground. After about an hour of crawling along no faster than they could have walked, the Jeep nosed into another clearing. There was a well-travelled trail coming into the clearing from the left—the same trail on which they had arrived at this same clearing an hour earlier.

"We've just made a big circle," Robby said.

"Yeah, so much for your *evidence of a trail*," Grant scolded. He pointed the Jeep back toward the hill again, stopped, set the parking brake and got out. He looked toward the sky, and then walked into the edge of the woods on the hillside. Robby followed.

Keith climbed out of the Jeep and came after them. "If you go up the hill a little to the left, it levels off," he said. "And then you go up a ways more and at the top you're looking out over several more hills and valleys."

"How do you know?" Robby asked.

"'Cause Dad and I walked it when we were out here hunting last year."

"Well, why didn't you say something before we ran around in circles?"

"I thought you knew where you were going."

"Well, that's the way we'll go this time," Grant concluded.

"Sounds more like what Cory described."

They boarded the Jeep and started up the hill. By this time, the sun had advanced a little, and when they could see it through the forest canopy, it did seem as though they were generally headed west. At the top of the ridge, Grant stopped the Jeep. Ahead lay hazy miles of ridges and valleys between them and the distant horizon. "This looks more like it," Grant said. His heart raced with excitement. This was the wilderness he was hoping to encounter.

The sure-footed little Jeep plunged down off the ridge. As Grant threaded his way westward, the landscape changed at nearly every turn. One minute, they were engulfed by a sea of tall prairie grass, and the next they dipped down into a jungle-like valley. The familiar geography surrounding Wellington had long since disappeared behind them. Time and space had taken on different dimensions: space seemed limitless, and time was something to be used, not saved. Things that seemed important just hours ago seemed insignificant now, as if this were a new beginning in a new and different world.

Bouncing along through the pathless terrain, they counted and crossed four ridges. As they approached the crest of number five, a tough climb over rugged, rocky ground, their anticipation peeked; just beyond the fifth ridge is where they should encounter a stream—Silver Creek—and just beyond that should be the hilltop where a thriving city once was the home for hundreds of people.

But somehow, it didn't seem right. In his journal, Cory had never mentioned terrain this rough or difficult. Grant maneuvered the Jeep defiantly to the crest, and then cautiously crept down the other side. Partway down, his instinct told him to stop; the slope ahead was getting too steep.

They continued on foot down the slope toward the sound of rushing water. They had found Silver Creek, but when their eyes connected with it, they knew they must have gone off course. The stream rushed along rocky rapids in a deep ravine between steep, rocky banks.

"This can't be where he crossed the creek," Grant said. "No way *any* four-wheeler could cross here."

"Which way d'ya think we need to go?" Keith asked.

Robby scratched his head. "The gunman that shot Buck Paxton supposedly came upstream in a canoe," he said. "Nobody could canoe in a stream like this."

"I think we should follow it downstream," Grant suggested.

"I think you're right," the others agreed.

Following the top of the ridge was impossible; too many large boulders blocked the way and sheer drop-offs prevented getting around them. Backtracking into the last valley, Grant picked his way to another possible passage over the top. It was an easy climb and descent, but Silver Creek had angled away to the opposite side of the valley. By the time they reached it again, another hour had passed since the first sighting. Dusk was slowly approaching.

"This doesn't look like it, either," Robby said after they battled their way through a field of willow saplings and bottomland mud. Silver Creek was a little tamer there, but the banks consisted of mud... and more mud; nothing like Cory had described, and the hills on the other side just didn't seem right, either.

"Let's try to get downstream a little farther before it gets dark," Grant said. "We can find a place to camp for the night, and then try again in the morning."

"Good," Keith cried out. "I'm getting hungry."

They were all getting hungry. Evening shadows were gobbling up everything in sight, but they managed to find a dry, level spot between the woods and the creek to set up camp. Robby rounded up some firewood with the use of a flashlight while Grant and Keith constructed the dome tent and aired up the mattress in the illumination of the Jeep's headlights. They stayed so busy for a little while getting everything together for a night's stay and getting a campfire started, they didn't have time to fear the possible dangers that lurked in the darkness. They didn't think about what a remote, forgotten place they had delivered themselves into, or the deadly, hideous reputation it had gained in years past. Instead, they found comfort in each other's company, soothing warmth from the fire, delight in the hot dogs that were filling their bellies, and a sense of freedom they had never experienced before.

So far, their attempt at finding haunted Silver Spring and Tanglewood Lodge had not been too successful. But for the moment, it really didn't matter.

FOURTEEN

They were all thankful that they had found a dry place to camp; with the heavy rainfall the day before, that could have become an issue. Since their last encounter with Silver Creek where they experienced the mud, climbing to higher ground back in the hills certainly seemed likely. They had apparently just stumbled into a marshy pocket there, but here they were perfectly safe and dry.

Once their hunger was satisfied, they lay back and enjoyed the night. No moon made for absolute darkness, and the inky black sky, it seemed, held more stars here. The creatures of the night talked to each other: somewhere a distant coyote howled, and another answered; an owl hoo-hoo-hooted and another returned with a similar call. The smell of the campfire smoke mingled with the piney scent of this territory that had remained undisturbed by any man for decades.

Robby, Keith, and Grant had not forgotten the reason for their mission. They no longer knew exactly where they were, although they would not concede to the idea of being lost. Silver Spring and Tanglewood Lodge—if it still existed after all these years—couldn't be far away.

"Why did it take us so long to get this far?" Keith asked. "If I read it right, it didn't take Cory Brockway this long to reach Silver Spring."

"He just happened to take the right route when he found it the first time," Grant replied. He used a stick to scratch some lines in the dirt by the fire to represent Silver Creek and the route they had followed. "He started out from the same place we did, but he must've followed a different line. We ended up here," Grant said, pointing to the spot where their path and Silver Creek met. "Cory reached the creek farther downstream the first time." He scratched a line from the starting point at Highway 43 to Silver Creek, forming a triangle in the dirt. "He came a much shorter route than we did."

"We need to find *his route*," Keith said.

"We will," Grant responded. "When we go back we'll cut off all this distance." He pointed to his map in the dirt again. "Don't worry... I'll find the shorter route."

"Robby," Grant said. "Did your Grandpa ever mention what happened to the guy who went to jail for shooting Cory's friend... what was his name?"

"The shooter's name was Sinclair," Robby said. "But Grandpa Vic didn't think it was him."

"Why? Did he ever say?"

"He knew that Cory and Buck and him had been friends... he just didn't think Sinclair would've done it. And he never said what happened to him after prison."

"So it was Sinclair's grandfather who was one of the looters that escaped the gunfight between McDowell   Junior and Clancy Crane."

"Yeah."

"Think he knew about the silver treasure?"

"Don't know, but I doubt it. *No one* knew about it 'cept Clancy."

"How about Cory's friend, Buck?" Keith said.

"Buck had gone back to Washington with his parents by the time Cory discovered the clues in Clancy's journal," Robby said. "I never saw any indication that they stayed in contact much after they parted ways after the trial. I don't think Cory ever told him about it."

"So you're still confident that *we're the only living beings* who have ever known about it?"

"Yeah."

"Well, I'm getting tired," Grant said. He started taking off his shirt. "I'm goin' to bed."

"Me too," said Robby.

Keith wasn't really sleepy, but he didn't want to sit out there in the dark all alone, so he followed the other two into the tent.

Shaded from the early morning sun by the tall stand of pines behind the tent, cool air wrapped pleasantly around the campsite. Keith was the first awake and out of the tent to find his way into the woods. When he came into the open again, he gazed out across the stream and the land beyond; they had not seen it last night in the dark. On the opposite bank of the creek stood a small clump of trees enveloped in a low layer of fog blanketing a narrow prairie. Rising up beyond that, the crest of a tree-covered ridge was just beginning to capture the first early rays of sunlight. As he paralleled the creek something glinted a sunray, catching Keith's eye. He stopped to peer at the distant hilltop.

"ROBBY! GRANT!" he called out. "Wake up! Come out here!"

"We're awake," Grant called back. He came crawling out of the tent, Robby right behind him. They, too, headed for the woods to take care of morning business.

Their reaction was much the same as Keith's had been. Robby and Grant stared in awe at the ridge across the creek.

"This is it," Robby said softly.

Grant stepped closer to the creek and then started walking slowly alongside the swift, silent current. Only twenty yards from the camp, the banks on either side of the creek met the water with a gradual slope of natural gravel and sand. The stream was about thirty feet wide, clean and clear, not more than a foot or eighteen inches deep.

"This must be where Cory crossed," he said.

Robby and Keith were beside him, too, surveying the possibilities. "He did have to wade across one time," Robby said. "He could certainly do it here."

"Well, we don't have to wade," Grant said. "The Jeep'll go across here… easy."

FIFTEEN

The climb up the side of the ridge was steeper than it looked from a distance. Now they knew why Cory had always left his Bronco at the bottom and went up on foot. They didn't search for the easier path that Cory had eventually discovered; getting to the plateau and viewing this mysterious place carried top priority.

"I saw something shiny glittering in the sun this morning," Keith said. "I think it was over that way." He pointed to their right, and the three continued on in that direction, occasionally tripping over flat, square stones that were apparently the remains of building foundations. A few small trees had sprouted here and there, but most of the level ridge top that stretched out for at least a mile or more was covered with prairie grass and clumps of weeds.

But there it was. Tanglewood Lodge. A two-story, tan brick box that had not only survived a fire that destroyed the rest of the town, it had withstood all the rigors that Mother Nature had thrown at it over the course of more than a century. The name painted across the upper front wall was all but wind-worn away, but the verandah that Cory Brockway had described in his journal remained intact.

"How could this possibly still be here?" Keith asked as he pounded his fist against a pillar holding up the porch roof.

Grant inspected. "It's made mostly of redwood and cedar," he said. "They intended for it to last."

The boys walked slowly around the entire structure, thoroughly amazed with its condition. Doors and windows were all in place, not a single pane of glass broken or missing.

"How can this be?" Robby said. "It's like someone has been taking care of it."

But there were no tracks; no trampled-down grass; no sign that any person had been there since Cory Brockway in 1968.

"We should look inside," Grant said.

"Think it's safe?" Keith questioned.

"Are you saying that because of ghosts... or the possibility of the floor caving in?"

Robby was already at the front door. "Be careful of the broken boards," he instructed the others, pointing to the verandah deck. He pulled the door open. The hinges squealed loudly in protest.

A hundred years' worth of dust had settled on everything. Numerous broken whiskey bottles lay scattered on the floor among splintered wooden chairs and tables. Part of a shattered mirror hung on the far wall behind a long mahogany bar. In one corner stood a rusted pot-belly stove, and in the opposite corner was the old upright piano that Cory Brockway had written about. The scene was just as Clancy Crane had described it right after he told of a Sheriff's posse that had loaded everything in wagons while he watched in hiding.

Robby and Grant carefully stepped down the hallway toward the rear of the building, looking in all the now empty chambers that had been dining rooms, gambling halls, storerooms, kitchen, laundry, and in the very back, the living quarters of the proprietor's family. When they exited the rear door, they realized that Keith was not with them. They went back through, thinking he must be lingering somewhere, but they emerged from the front without a trace of him anywhere. As they stood dumbfounded in front of the ancient edifice, more squealing hinges nearly drove them out of their skin.

"Hey, guys!" they heard Keith call out. There he was, leaning out from the only second floor window on the front side of the hotel. "You should see the view from up here," he said. "It's fantastic."

"What are you doing up there?" Robby yelled.

"Checking out the upstairs."

"What's up there?"

"A lot of empty rooms... nothing, really, but the view is great!"

Grant was curious. He headed to the front door and just inside he started cautiously up the grand staircase. Robby followed closely behind. At the front window where Keith waited for them, they gazed out on the plateau. From there they could see nearly the entire area where the town had once been. Off to their right, the land sloped down to where the railroad depot had been, and the faint evidence of rusted tracks lay in the tall grass. Following counter-clockwise around the perimeter of the plateau, they recognized the region that Clancy had identified as "beyond the dead line" where all the undesirables—the bums and the carpet baggers and the tramps lived—and on the slopes that fell away at the far end of the town site was where the silver smelter furnaces and the headquarters for the mining company had been.

For a couple of hundred feet out from the front of the hotel, from their elevated vantage point, the rock outlines of building foundations were visible, lying in a grid pattern that clearly identified the layout of that portion of the town. They hadn't noticed that at ground level, as the tall grass had kept it hidden.

"There," Robby said. "We can see where the streets were. We should be able to figure out where Oliver took the silver bars."

But once they were on the ground again and tried to follow what they thought were the streets, they soon found themselves in a state of mass confusion.

"What we need is a map," Robby said.

"Maybe the Historical Society has one." Keith offered.

"Better not go asking for a map there. It's best we keep this to ourselves," Robby insisted.

"We could draw out our own..."

"We'll be here all summer just getting all the measurements."

"If we could get up high enough looking down on it, like we did from the hotel window, all the building foundations would show up, and we could draw a map from that," Grant suggested.

"Yeah, and how are we gonna get up there? A sky hook?"

They all thought a few moments.

"How about a helicopter?" Grant said.

"Right," Robby laughed. "Where are we gonna get a helicopter... and a pilot willing to fly us there?"

"No, no, no," Grant said. "Remember the radio control model helicopter my dad built for me? For my fourteenth birthday?"

"Oh, yeah," Keith said. "You used to get so mad 'cause I could always fly it better than you could."

"Well, Hot Shot... d'ya think you can still fly it?"

"Don't know why not," Keith replied with confidence.

"We can rig Dad's remote control camera on it," Grant further explained his idea. "You can fly the chopper while I operate the camera—we can get all the pictures we need to make a map."

"Yeah," Robby said with a fountain of renewed enthusiasm. "A lot of things might be visible from above that we can't see on the ground... and we can use Clancy's journal to locate all the buildings."

"And Oliver's hiding spot."

Sixteen

They spent the rest of the day extending their search over the entire Silver Spring site, no idea of what they might find. As they weren't trained, expert archaeologists, they wouldn't know what to look for, where to look for it, or what to do with it once they found it. It was quite certain, now, that the treasure they sought would not be easily found; the area that Silver Spring had occupied was much larger than they had expected. But Robby placed his confidence in Clancy's journal to narrow the search area, and possibly isolate a few hot spots.

Grant's idea to employ his helicopter and camera for aerial photographs was brilliant; it would help them prepare a map so they could better identify the places Clancy described, and maybe even spot a few things that might otherwise go undetected.

All that, of course, would mean additional trips to Silver Spring. They would have to come at least once more to fly the helicopter and shoot the photographs, and again to make their search after preparing the map. But for now, they would see what they could see, and maybe, with a little stroke of luck, they might stumble onto something good.

After a hearty lunch of more hot dogs and potato chips, the boys combed the upper end of the ridge nearest the old hotel. It seemed most logical that their probe should produce better results there. If Oliver *had* hidden the silver bars in a building, the building would have been somewhere in this part of town. And if Grant's theory was correct about the wind and rain dispersing the ashes that covered them at the time of the fire, they might be somewhere in the vicinity, now hidden only by the tall grass and weeds.

About fifty yards from Tanglewood, Robby kicked through the weeds and grass inside the perimeter of one foundation while Keith and Grant hunted another. Keith abruptly halted and froze where he stood.

"What's wrong?" Grant asked when he noticed Keith's strange expression.

"Did you hear that?"

"Hear what?" Grant said.

"Sounded like..."

"Like what?"

"Like... music... listen. There it is again."

Grant cocked his head to one side, listening. After a few seconds of intense concentration, he, too, could just barely hear what sounded like the tinkling of a piano.

Robby noticed the strange lack of movement in his two friends. "Did you find something?" he called out.

Grant just shook his head no. "Listen," he whispered loudly.

It took only a few seconds for Robby to zero in on the faint but distinct sound. He looked at his wristwatch, and then to the front of Tanglewood. Without another word he started slowly and cautiously toward the ancient building. Grant and Keith gave up their search through the weeds and followed him. Ten feet from the hotel's verandah, they stopped. More distinctly, now, the melodious resonance continued. Keith took a step forward but Grant held him back.

Seconds later a gunshot was heard, and then another, and then the sound of shattering glass.

And then the piano stopped. All was silent.

"Three-fifteen. Just like Cory described," Robby said softly.

"Y-you don't think we're just imagining all this, do you?" Keith said.

"Did you hear a piano?" Grant asked.

Keith nodded.

"Yeah," Robby said.

"Did you hear two gunshots?"

Robby and Keith both nodded.

"Did you hear glass breaking?"

"Yes."

"Both of you heard the same sounds I heard," Grant concluded. "I don't think we'd all imagine the same thing all at the same time."

"And don't you remember?" Robby added. "Cory heard all the same stuff, too... several times. And it was always about three-fifteen."

Keith stepped up onto the verandah and scrupulously pulled open the door.

"See anything?" Grant asked.

"Nothing that wasn't here this morning."

"The place really *is* haunted," Robby mumbled.

"Yeah," Grant replied. "Now, if only we could get *Oliver* to show up..."

SEVENTEEN

With a whole different outlook, now, on this place called Silver Spring, they broke camp about noon on Sunday. Grant pointed the Jeep into the hills and followed his instinct.

Over the second ridge, Robby asked Keith, "Did you remember to close that upstairs window?"

"Yes," Keith replied. "Did you lock the back door and turn out the lights?"

Grant laughed at Keith's sarcasm, but Robby was thinking more seriously. To him, preservation of that old building seemed important. Keeping the weather out was a vital factor.

"Do you think there's a chance we might be wasting our time?" Keith asked.

Robby hesitated. "I don't think so. Cory Brockway had some strong feelings about this... and so do I."

"But if Cory had such strong feelings about it, why didn't he try to find the treasure?"

"He discovered the clues too late. I think he just ran out of time and opportunities."

"So when are we going back?" Keith asked.

"The whirly bird hasn't been in the air since last summer," Grant said. "I'll have to get it all checked over... and I'll have to figure out how to rig the camera."

"I can help you with that," Keith offered.

Over two more ridges they ran onto their tracks made on the outbound trip.

"See?" Grant declared. "Told you I'd find the shorter route."

It *was* a shorter route—less than half of the initial distance they had travelled on the way out—and much less demanding on the vehicle. The hills weren't quite as steep and much less rugged terrain. All the way, Grant made mental notes of the landmarks so he could follow the same trail again.

EIGHTEEN

There was a large room in the Kraemer basement—the "man cave"—where all the Kraemer men could escape the real world to enjoy a little solitude without any outside interference. All the comforts and necessities for survival were contained within its walls: couch, TV and DVD player, stereo, game table, refrigerator stocked with plenty of beer, soft drinks, and frozen pizzas, coffee maker, microwave, pizza oven, and it even had its own bathroom complete with shower. Shelves built into one wall held an array of books, magazines, CDs, DVDs, and board games. At the far end was a workbench with a variety of tools and gadgets hung on pegboard hooks above it. In closets they knew right where to find golf clubs, tennis rackets, baseball bats and gloves, basketballs, footballs, softballs, and now that young Kevin had been admitted as a member, soccer balls had been recently added to the collection. A six-by-eight table occupied the center of the room where the HO scale railroad and miniature town still received quite a bit of attention. On its very own shelf, high on the wall behind the model railroad, sat Grant's helicopter and all the accessories.

When Grant and Keith opened the door to the man cave Monday afternoon, the recessed ceiling fluorescents lit the soft hue of maple paneling; Earl had installed the automatic sensors because boys often forget to turn out the lights when they leave. The room glowed with friendly, inviting warmth; Keith loved this room—he was trying to replicate it at the Bradley house, but so far, he hadn't yet quite achieved the same effects.

"Where's Robby?" Grant asked.

"Running some errands for Mrs. G," Keith replied. "He'll be over later."

They carefully hoisted the helicopter down from the shelf and set it on the workbench.

Grant's helicopter wasn't a toy; it was a serious-minded model pilot's aircraft. Over three feet long nose to tail and nearly four-foot rotor diameter, it looked like a real helicopter, just smaller. With collective pitch rotors—unlike the fixed-pitch like most beginners would start with—it controlled and flew much like a real helicopter, more difficult to learn, but a much more stable craft with superior maneuverability. Earl had been more impressed with the realism, and he was confident that his son could master the more complicated flight controller.

From the very beginning, Keith had sat in on all the video pilot self-training courses and read all the manuals. He was there when Earl instructed Grant about pre-flight inspections and maintenance, and he was there at the deserted softball field when they made the first test flight. With a little practice, Grant could maneuver the bird fairly well, but when Keith got his turn to try it, it seemed he was a natural; he had the controls mastered in a very short time and he could fly that bird like a pro.

"Have any idea how to mount the camera?" Keith asked.

"I think we can clamp the head from a camera tripod to the landing gear runners," Grant advised. "The head   pivots so we can point the camera in any direction... of course, we need it to point straight down."

"But isn't that gonna throw the weight of the chopper off balance?"

"The gyro should compensate for that. We'll take it out to the ball field and try it out."

By the time Robby arrived, Grant and Keith had disassembled the tripod and they were attaching the pivot head to the helicopter landing gear with a small C-clamp.

"Is it gonna work?" Robby asked. "It won't come loose and fall off?"

"I'll tether the camera with some nylon cord... just in case,"

Grant said. He opened a cupboard door, retrieved the digital camera, and threaded it onto the tripod mounting screw. With a little adjusting, the camera was positioned between the landing gear runners, the lens pointed straight down.

"Perfect," Grant said. He smiled with satisfaction. "Now, I'll check out everything else. The batteries can charge up tonight, and by tomorrow morning we can go to the ball field and make a test flight."

"I have a dentist appointment tomorrow morning," Keith said. "Better plan on after lunch."

NINETEEN

Karen Bradley and Phyllis Gladstone planned a whole day of shopping together Tuesday morning on the phone during breakfast. Now that Keith had his own car, he could get himself across town to his dentist appointment. Phyllis had nothing to do that was so important that it couldn't wait until another day. It would be *their* day out on the town.

Robby and Grant decided to go to Abbey's Café and Keith would meet them there when he was finished at the dentist's office. Because it was long before the lunch hour began, there were empty parking spaces right in front. The yellow Mustang occupied one.

After they ordered two glasses of iced tea and informed the waitress that they would wait for Keith to arrive before ordering meals, Robby placed a pad of drawing paper on the table. "We need some sort of system to take these pictures," he told Grant. He drew a long wide oval shape to represent the area on the ridge. "We know that Silver Spring had a Main Street. Did it run across the ridge... or the length of it?"

"Makes more sense that it ran the length of the ridge," Grant replied. He drew a line lengthwise down the center of the oval. "Clancy wrote that the hotel was at the corner of Main and Connor Street, and that Connor Street was the last street on that end of town."

"Right... but Clancy mentions seeing Oliver on other street names, too."

Just then the iced tea arrived. "Anything else I can get for you now?" the waitress asked.

"Not right now, thank you," Grant said. "When Keith gets here, we'll order some lunch."

As the waitress delivered coffee and water to another table, Grant continued. "Oliver probably didn't use the same route every night."

"Yeah," Robby affirmed. "And when Clancy saw him on some of the other streets was when Clancy was on his way to the market square. Oliver was probably avoiding being seen by other people."

"What's important..." Grant said, "...is knowing which direction on which street Oliver was going when the bag was full."

"All we have to go on are the names of business places where Clancy saw him passing by."

It was just past noon when Keith came in. The whole place was filling up fast.

"Hey, Keith... how'd it go at the dentist?"

"He said my wisdom teeth will have to come out sometime soon, but I told him I don't have time for that now." Keith eyed the drawing pad. "What are you drawing?"

"We were just discussing how to go about taking the pictures at Silver Spring," Robby said.

"I think we'll just start at the southern end... where the smelter was," Grant said. He drew some lines lengthwise across the oval. "It'll take several passes from end to end to get it all."

"How high is the chopper gonna be?" Keith asked.

"I think about fifty or sixty feet," Grant replied.

"Fly higher... say... a hundred feet," Keith said. "It'll mean fewer pictures 'cause the camera will shoot a larger area, and it'll take less time. Remember... we'll only have about twenty-eight minutes of flying time with two fully charged battery packs. Maybe less, 'cause the camera weight is gonna make the chopper work a little harder."

"Good point," Grant said. "But I found an inverter in Dad's stuff. I can hook it up to the Jeep battery and recharge the chopper batteries if we need more flying time."

Robby had another suggestion. "If you can fire that camera

from a longer distance, even higher would be okay. We can enlarge the photos on the computer."

"That's a good idea. We could probably get the entire area in about fifteen or twenty shots."

"You guys ready to order?" the waitress asked.

"Ranch Burgers and Curly Fries for all of us," Robby responded.

"And another iced tea, please," Keith added.

TWENTY

Glad to see that no one was using the softball field, Grant pulled his Jeep right up to the backstop fence. Keith carried the helicopter like it was a baby out to the center of the field; Grant brought the flight controller and the remote control for the camera.

Keith had been right: the weight of the camera did affect the performance of the chopper, but with a little higher than normal motor speed the craft lifted off smoothly. Keith flew it slowly around the field a few times at low altitude to get the feel of the controls again and to make sure everything was operating properly. When it felt comfortably safe, he gained altitude, continuing a wide spiral upward until the chopper reached an altitude well over a hundred feet.

"Wanna try the camera at this altitude?" he asked Grant.

"Sure," Grant said and pointed to the far side of the field. "Fly over those houses... slow... and then come this way. I'll try about four or five shots."

Keith maneuvered the chopper in a wide arc past left field, beyond the perimeter of the park, banked right, and hovered with the nose pointed toward the field. "Whenever you're ready," he said to Grant.

Grant pointed the camera remote control toward the helicopter. "Okay... come this way slow... and try to stay at the same altitude."

The chopper moved slowly toward the field; Grant clicked off the fifth frame when the craft was right overhead. "Take it up another fifty feet or so..."

They repeated the same procedure at the higher altitude and then Keith brought the bird down for a perfect, gentle touchdown in the grass just behind second base.

The first sequence of five pictures at the lower altitude overlapped so much that two shots would have covered the same area, and the same was true of the second sequence at the higher level, but from what they could determine on just the small camera display screen, the pictures were clear and seemed to display the features on the ground with enough detail, including three boys, heads tilted back, staring upward at the camera.

"Let's go home and download these on the computer," Grant said. "I think this is gonna work."

Viewing the pictures on the computer monitor screen gave Grant a better understanding of the distance the helicopter should advance between shots. He printed the first and last frames of each sequence, lined up the overlap and then Scotch taped them together. What they had with the second sequence was a perfect aerial view of a block of house roofs, the softball diamond with the three of them standing on the pitcher's mound, and the parking lot with a Patriot Blue Jeep.

"This is great," Robby commented. "Better than the satellite photo maps on the internet."

"Yeah," Grant said. "I had the camera set at the highest resolution and the fastest shutter speed. If we have a nice, clear day, we'll get all the detail we need."

TWENTY-ONE

Kevin Kraemer was arriving home after summer camp on Friday. Because Earl and Judy wouldn't be back from their vacation yet, Grant had been instructed to pick him up from the school parking lot where the bus would drop off the group. He was only thirteen—old enough to be left home alone for a day, perhaps, but mischievous enough not to be trusted alone for the whole weekend.

"We could take him along," Robby suggested. He had always liked Kevin and had considered him one of the gang, even if he was five years younger.

"There won't be enough room in my Jeep for all the camping gear, *four* of us, *and* the helicopter," Grant said.

"Sure there is," Robby protested. "Kevin's not that big... we can squeeze him in somehow."

"I don't know..."

"Well, you can't just lock him in the attic. There's laws against that."

Grant laughed. "Could he stay at your house?"

"Don't you remember? Keith's parents and my parents are going to Castleburg for the weekend to see some stage show... Mr. and Mrs. K would've gone, too, if they weren't on vacation."

Keith sauntered across the back yard, slid open the patio door, came in and sat on the breakfast bar stool next to Robby. "Your Jeep is dirty," he said. "Our cars are kinda dusty, too... we should wash 'em all."

"Would you care if Kevin comes with us camping this weekend?" Grant asked Keith.

73

"Do we have enough room?"

"We'll have to *make* room," Robby said. "All the moms and dads will be gone. Kevin's coming home from camp on Friday and Grant doesn't think we should leave him home alone."

"I guess it's okay with me," Keith replied. "But does this mean we have to cut him in on the treasure?"

Grant and Robby laughed.

"We don't tell him what we're doing out there," Grant said.

"But you *know* he's gonna ask questions."

"We just tell him that we're mapping out the old town... and that won't be a lie."

"Okay... if you say so. Now. Are we gonna wash our dirty cars?"

The Grand Prix was voted taxi of the day to pick up Kevin at the school. The Jeep was loaded down with camping gear and a helicopter, and Kevin would have a backpack and a large duffel bag. He was expecting to see his brother and a Jeep, so Keith had to call out his name and wave to get his attention. Kevin pushed his way through the pack of rowdy twelve- and thirteen-year-old boys who had just completed a summer soccer training camp, glad to escape the discipline and eager to start doing the things youngsters usually do during summer vacation. "Hey, Kev," Keith greeted him as he opened the trunk.

"Hey, Punky," the boy returned. Besides the moms, Kevin was still allowed to call Keith by his nickname, but that would soon come to an end. "How come you're here? Where's Grant?"

"He's mowing the lawn."

"Couldn't that wait?" Kevin asked, as if he felt hurt because his brother didn't come to meet him.

"No," Keith said. "You see, he wanted to get it done before tomorrow... we're all going camping, and you're coming along."

"Really?" Kevin beamed. "You mean with tents and sleeping bags and campfires?"

"Yup. But I s'pose you've had enough of that for a while."

"Are you kidding? We slept in a dorm, lights out by nine, ate in a cafeteria, and we got to have a bonfire only one night the whole time we were there."

"Sounds rough. Life of an athlete, huh? How was the training?"

"Oh, the training was good. We all practiced together, and then we split up in teams and played regular games. It was fun. So, where are we going camping?"

"Out in the Wilderness... we're roughin' it."

"Cool."

TWENTY-TWO

With a little rearranging and creative packing, Robby and Kevin occupied the rear seat of the Jeep with duffels and sleeping bags stacked between them, and the helicopter perched on top of that, the tail rotor extended forward between Grant's and Keith's shoulders.   Once again, there was no ceremonious send-off because it was such an ordinary weekend activity for the boys. Phyllis didn't even see anything unusual about the helicopter; boys like to play with their toys.

"We'll be back Sunday night from Castleburg," she told them as the four boys piled into the Jeep. "Be careful and have fun."

"We will," and then the three boy choir plus one sang out, "Thanks Mom."

Grant was having no difficulty following the same trail back to Silver Spring. Much of the way, the tracks from their previous trip were still visible, and where the trail seemed nonexistent, his memory of landmarks was still fresh in his mind.

Kevin, though, was getting more than curious during the lengthy ride through the hills. "Do you know where you're going?" he asked his brother.

"Yeah... we were out here last weekend."

"Why are you going so far out? We've passed lots of good spots to camp."

"'Cause we're going to a particular place."

"Why?"

"It's a good place to fly the chopper."

"Why do you have this thing along, anyway?"

"Kevin?" Grant said sternly. "I'll stop and make you get out and walk the rest of the way if you don't quit asking so many questions."

Even though Robby knew Grant wouldn't make his brother walk, he reached over and put his hand on the boy's shoulder. "Don't worry about it now," he said. "I'll explain it all to you when we get out there... okay?"

When they arrived at Silver Creek Grant asked, "Should we camp in the same spot? Or should we go across and find a place closer to the hill?"

Robby and Keith pondered a few moments, and then they both agreed that camping closer to the hill seemed more practical—they wouldn't have to cross the creek to get to their campsite.

Kevin's knuckles turned white holding onto the back of the driver's seat as Grant eased the Jeep into the water at the crossing. "What are you doing?" he yelled.

Robby calmed him down. "It's okay, Kev... we've crossed here a few times... it's okay."

Grant, Keith, and Robby felt little or no apprehension about entering into *Mack's territory* this time; they *had* experienced uneasiness during their prior visit; they *had* encountered a rather strange occurrence at the hotel that remained unexplainable. But it also seemed rather harmless and non-threatening. No ghoulish creatures had jumped out from a dark corner to attack them; no strangely hidden booby traps caught them unaware—just the sounds of piano music and gunshots. If anything else existed there on that hilltop, it was invisible and harmless. They had proven—just as Cory Brockway had proven in 1967 and 1968—that the legend of Mack, the fiendish, murderous ghost that everyone feared was really nothing to fear at all.

Kevin, however, was feeling regret for his participation on the trip as the Jeep crawled through tall prairie grass approaching the hill. He looked as if he might cry when he gazed upon the area where his weekend guardians intended to set up camp.

"What did you expect?" Grant said, noticing his brother's apparent displeasure. "Swimming pool and mini-golf?"

"N-no, but..."

"Well, we're out in the wilderness now. You'll like it... you'll see."

"I don't know..."

"This is nature... where's your sense of adventure? Now, go help Robby find some firewood."

Robby, too, noticed Kevin's sour response to the destination. He grabbed the hatchet from the Jeep. "Hey, Kev," he said cheerfully. "Let's go look for firewood. Grant and Punky can set up the tent."

Kevin appeared grateful to go with Robby, perhaps to distance himself from his brother for a while. Grant wasn't offering him the right pacifier at the moment; maybe Robby would.

"This isn't really so bad," Robby told him when they were part-way up the hillside cutting some dead branches fallen to the ground. "Kinda nice, actually... no parents telling you what to do... eat and drink pop whenever you want... take a leak wherever you happen to be—as long as it's away from our camp..."

Kevin giggled and smiled just a little. Already, Robby was helping him feel better about his temporary accommodations.

"We found a good swimming hole in the creek," Robby said pointing downstream. "Gets pretty hot out here."

"But I didn't bring any swimming trunks."

"Who needs 'em? Skinny dippin' is okay out here... no one but us for miles around."

Kevin gazed in the direction Robby had pointed toward the swimming hole, showing signs of approval and mild interest.

"And I'll even show you a haunted house."

Kevin's face seemed to light up when *"haunted house"* finally registered. "Really? There's a haunted house out here?" he said, a generous portion of excitement coloring his words.

"Yeah. Up on top of the ridge there used to be a town over a hundred years ago. Only thing left now is one old brick house... well, actually it was a hotel. We heard music coming from it last weekend... looked all through it but there was nobody inside."

"You went *inside?*"

"Yeah."

"Cooooool," Kevin sighed. "Can we go see it?"

"Later," Robby said. "I'm getting hungry and we need to get a fire going to roast hot dogs."

TWENTY-THREE

Now that Kevin's attitude had been properly adjusted, they each gathered up an arm-load of wood and headed back to the campsite. The tent was up and sleeping bags tossed in on the inflated air mattress. Keith found some rocks from the hillside while Grant cleared a spot and dug out a fire pit. Within twenty minutes the four of them were standing around the fire consuming a massive amount of hot dogs.

"Are we gonna try to shoot some pictures today?" Keith asked. He was anxious to go flying.

"Sure," Grant answered. "If we can't finish before we run out of battery power, the batteries can charge up for tomorrow."

"What are you taking pictures of?" Kevin asked.

"The land up on the hill," Grant replied.

"Why?"

"We're making a map."

"A map of what?"

"Old building foundations."

"Why?"

"Because we want to."

Robby could see that Grant was running short on   patience with his little brother. He collared Kevin with one arm and started walking him away where he couldn't bombard his brother with irritating questions. "You see, Kev," he started to explain. "We have this old diary that was written by a guy who lived here."

"Where'd you get it?" Kevin asked.

"I found it in my Grandpa Vic's stuff up in our attic." Robby went on to explain that the journal described in detail the location of all the business places that were in the town and the names of some of the streets, and that they were going to create a map.

"So, what's the helicopter for?" Kevin quizzed.

"There's a remote control camera mounted on it. Keith is going to fly the chopper over the area and Grant will shoot the pictures."

"Why from the helicopter?"

"'Cause the tall grass hides everything when you're looking at it from the ground. Looking straight down, all the building foundation rocks will show and the pictures will give us the whole layout."

"Cool. When can we go to the haunted house?"

"We'll check out the house while they're taking the pictures... we'll just stay out of their way."

"Cool."

They watched quietly while Keith and Grant performed a pre-flight inspection of the helicopter. When the aviators seemed to be ready, they carried the craft to the hill and started up the steep incline, but it proved a difficult task.

"Why don't you just fly it up there?" Kevin suggested innocently, seeing how much trouble they were having.

Grant and Keith exchanged dumbfounded stares, and then brought the bird back down on the level ground.

"I'll go up on top and fly it from there," Keith said. A few minutes later he called out from the top of the ridge, "CLEAR!" He wanted to be sure everyone was safely away from the helicopter; spinning rotors could do a lot of damage, even if it was only a model. The motor started and the rotor blades sliced the warm summer air; Keith gradually increased the pitch and the chopper lifted gracefully off the valley floor, buzzed into space like a giant bumble bee, high above the boys watching from below, swooped over to the ridge top and disappeared behind the trees as Keith quickly set it down again to conserve the needed battery power for the photo session.

Robby, Grant and Kevin scrambled to the top of the hill. In a short time, Keith had the chopper in the air again at an altitude of about 150 feet. It hovered at the southern perimeter of the site where the silver smelter furnaces and chimneys lay in heaps of rubble. Grant began clicking pictures as the bird progressed slowly and steadily northward.

"Can we go see the haunted house now?" Kevin begged.

"Sure," Robby replied. "There's not much we can do here." He pointed Kevin toward the old hotel.

"D'ya think we'll hear the music again?" Kevin asked as they tramped through the tall grass.

"Don't know… prob'ly not 'til later this afternoon."

"Why this afternoon?"

"'Cause that's when it's always heard… about three-fifteen in the afternoon."

"How do you know that?"

"It's in the old journal I got from my Grandpa's stuff… written by another guy who was out here several times."

"When was he here?"

"In nineteen-sixty-seven."

"Wow! That was a long time ago."

"Yeah… almost forty years."

"Why did he come out here?"

"He just accidently stumbled onto it."

"Doesn't anyone else know about this place?"

Robby hesitated. "Yeah, there are other people who know about it, but no one ever comes here."

"Why?"

"They're afraid to come because it's haunted."

"Why aren't you and Punky and my brother afraid of it?"

"Because we have the journals… and we know all the secrets."

"What secrets?"

They had reached Tanglewood Lodge and stood at the front verandah. Robby paused for a few moments, listening, just in case there was a chance he might hear the music. Nothing. A few birds squawked in the tree branches that hung over the old building and he could hear the buzz of the helicopter approaching from behind them, but no piano. He stepped up onto the verandah; Kevin, though, seemed a little hesitant to follow.

"C'mon, Kev," Robby coaxed. "It's okay... there's no reason to be afraid."

Kevin remained firmly planted on the ground while Robby pulled open the heavy wooden door; as usual, the rusty hinges squealed mercilessly; Kevin took a step backwards. Robby stepped inside, and rather than being left all alone, Kevin jumped onto the verandah. Robby heard his footsteps hastily following him through the doorway, and suddenly Kevin was by his side.

"See?" Robby said. "Nothing to be afraid of."

"Cool."

Keith had turned the chopper and was starting the next pass southward about a block west from the hotel. Robby and Kevin observed from the window close to the old   piano; Robby suddenly sensed an odd, uncertain feeling that *he* was being watched. He abruptly turned and scanned the interior of the spacious, dusty room.

"What's wrong?" Kevin asked.

"Oh... nothing," Robby replied. He held his breath, listening, looking one more time, and then he returned his attention to the helicopter and Keith through the window. Apparently, the chopper was losing power; Keith was signaling to Grant that he would bring it down for a landing to change the battery. When the craft was on the ground, Robby noticed Keith looking all around, as if he might have heard something out of the ordinary and was searching for its source. A minute later, he seemed to dismiss the search, and went to work installing the fresh battery pack in the helicopter. Grant joined him and checked the camera, reviewing a few of the aerial pictures on the camera LCD screen. A few more minutes passed and the chopper was in the air again, resuming the original flight pattern.

Kevin wanted to resume the tour of the old building. "What's down that hallway?" he asked. He had become so intrigued with the eerie confines that he had apparently forgotten his earlier line of questions ending with "*What secrets.*"

"A lot of empty rooms," Robby informed him. "They were probably dining rooms and gambling rooms, and one looks like it might have been a kitchen."

They continued down the hallway, gazing into each chamber, until they came to a stairway.

"Can we go upstairs?" Kevin inquired.

Robby remembered seeing the back staircase during the previous visit. Perhaps, this is where Keith had separated from him and Grant when he turned up missing. "Step carefully," he instructed Kevin. "The boards could be rotten and weak." He led the way cautiously up the darkened stairway.

At the top, light from the windows shone through the open room doorways, casting bright rectangular patches on the bare wood floorboards and the yellowed hallway walls. Large chunks of plaster had loosened and fallen from the walls and ceiling exposing the lath underneath; the paint was cracked and peeling. But considering its age and non-use for so many years, the place was remarkably well-preserved.

"What happened to the rest of the town?" Kevin asked.

"It was all destroyed by fire," Robby said.

"So… why is this place still here?"

"It was the only brick building in the whole town. According to the journals, all the windows and doors were closed tight because of bad weather, so no sparks ever got in. That's what saved it."

"How'd the fire start? Lightning?"

"No. A crazy man who killed the owner of this hotel started it."

"Why?"

"Vigilantes had him cornered in a horse barn. He lit the barn on fire to try to escape. The wind was so strong that day that the fire spread really fast. Nobody could do anything to stop it, and

84

the whole town burned down."

"So... did the guy get away?"

"Almost. The hotel owner's brother—who wrote one of the journals—snuck up behind him just before he got to the hotel and clubbed him on the head with a burning timber... killed him."

"Wow! This is *so* cool. A *real* haunted house! Wait 'til I tell my friends about this."

"You'd better not do that," Robby warned.

"Why?"

"We need to keep this a secret."

"You guys and your secrets," Kevin complained. "What're the secrets you guys know that nobody else knows?"

By that time they had passed by the front staircase and were peering out the only front window. Robby just caught a glimpse of the helicopter descending toward the campsite. When it had landed, Keith and Grant gazed over the hills; Keith extended his arm pointing toward the hillside to the east of Tanglewood. They were discussing something.

"Looks like they're done taking pictures," Robby said. "We'd better go down there."

Twenty-four

"Get all the pictures?" Robby inquired as he closed in on Keith and Grant.

"Everything up here," Grant replied. "But the battery is low in the chopper, and Keith wants to get some shots of the hillsides. We'll have to get them tomorrow."

"Did you find any ghosts in the hotel?" Keith wondered.

"No," Robby said. "But I got this weird feeling that someone was watching us."

Keith's grin changed to a stunned blank stare.

"Something wrong?" Robby asked.

Keith shook his head. "It's just kinda odd... 'cause... so did I... just before I landed the chopper for a fresh battery."

"D'ya s'pose there's somebody else out here?"

"Who *else* would *possibly* be out *here*?"

Robby hesitated. "Mack?" he said softly, as if he were either embarrassed or scared to speak the name. It had been Robby, early on, who had tried to convince Grant that Mack didn't exist; that Mack was simply a myth; that the college professor—by killing a treasure hunter in 1937—had provided the means for the myth to continue. All that Robby, Grant and Keith had learned from reading the old journals made that assumption seem quite logical. But now it seemed that Robby entertained second thoughts.

"Robby," Grant intervened. "There *is no Mack*... we've already proved that. Cory Brockway proved that. Let's not get ourselves all worked up over ghosts."

"But we've seen evidence... or at least we've *heard* evidence... the music coming from the hotel. How do you explain that?"

Grant pondered a moment, and then he offered a compromising comment. "McDowell wasn't a piano player."

Robby didn't have a reply. But regardless, he was considering his and Keith's earlier feelings with reverence.

"Who's Mack?" Kevin asked. He was entirely confused by the conversation.

"Nobody you need to worry about," Grant said.

Kevin turned to Robby. "Who's Mack?" he asked again, confident that Robby would give him a better answer.

"Just a myth," Robby replied. He didn't want Kevin to get upset again. "Just a ghost that everyone a long time ago thought was out here... nothing to be concerned about now."

"Is that one of the secrets?" Kevin quizzed.

"Yeah," Robby said. "That's one of the secrets."

Back at the campsite, Grant plugged the power inverter into the Jeep's cigarette lighter, and then plugged the helicopter battery charger into the inverter.

"Better start the Jeep once in a while," Keith suggested. "Let the Jeep battery recharge, too. We don't want to get stuck out here with a dead battery."

"Right," Grant agreed. "Now... anyone wanna go swimming? It's hot out here."

That seemed to be the best activity to pursue for the rest of the afternoon. They all hopped into the Jeep and Grant drove them through the tall prairie grass to the swimming hole. Even Kevin was enjoying the wilderness more, now.

Nothing could have been more refreshing; a dip in the stream was better than a cool shower after a hard game; this could last as long as they wanted it to last, and last it did until they realized their hunger about six o'clock. They went back to the campsite, consumed another massive dose of hot dogs and potato chips, and sat around their fire until the supply of firewood nearly depleted. As the light from the fire slowly faded, the boys gazed up to the hilltop through a cloud of spectral blue vapor—an emulsion of moonlight and wisps of fog settling in the valley. The hills, the trees, everything was bathed in a mystic blueness, the perfect atmosphere for the hoot of an owl and the cry of a coyote.

TWENTY-FIVE

Steamy morning fog softened the features of the hills surrounding the valley; the blueness had given way to the pink and orange glow filtering through from the eastern horizon. The air was fresh and clean, laden with wildflower fragrance, and in the morning stillness the silky murmur of water washing over the rocks in Silver Creek mingled with madrigal bird songs.

Keith paced around the camp, waiting impatiently for the sun to burn off the remaining haze, and for the others to finish a morning face wash at the creek, getting ready for another day. He had been up for a while and had already been for a swim after a sweaty night in the crowded tent; he felt refreshed, but that uneasy sensation of being under surveillance nagged him again this morning. It seemed rather foolish, but he couldn't discharge the notion from his head.

Together, he and Grant prepared the helicopter and camera for flight; with two freshly recharged battery packs they had another twenty-eight minutes of flying time to get more pictures.

With flashlights in hand, Robby and Kevin made the climb to Tanglewood. They would continue to explore and investigate on the ground while Keith and Grant surveyed from the air. Not long after they had entered the old hotel for another look around, something on the floor caught Kevin's eye; he pawed away the thick layer of dust from what appeared to be a large coin. He picked it up and rubbed it clean. The date on the silver dollar was 1893, and it was in remarkably good condition.

"Wow!" he exclaimed. "Robby! Look what I found."

Robby had checked the view from all the windows and had started the climb to the upper floor where the views were of better advantage. The awareness of being watched had once again stirred his senses earlier that morning, but he had not mentioned it as to cause alarm to the others. Perhaps it was just his paranoid imagination, he thought, but the sensation persisted. From the upper level windows he might get a glimpse of something—or someone—that was hidden from a lower angle of view, just like the rock foundations were hidden by the tall grass. Kevin's excitement, however, turned him back down the stairs.

Kevin met him at the bottom. "Look at this," he said, afire with exuberance. He held the coin for Robby to see.

"Where'd you find it?" Robby asked.

Kevin pointed. "Right over there... by that doorway."

Robby inspected the coin, noticing the date and its excellent condition. "Looks like you found a real treasure," he congratulated.

"Yeah," Kevin replied. "Maybe there's more... I'm gonna keep looking."

That would keep Kevin busy for a while; Robby continued back up the stairway.

Bright sunshine had burned away all the early morning fog; Grant was clicking photos of the hillsides as Keith flew the chopper around the outer perimeter of the town. Robby watched them for a while from the front window, and then turned to seek out other windows in other rooms. From many, the view was blocked by close trees, but one at the rear side of the building revealed a vista encompassing an abrupt rise of the terrain to the north, and a more gradual downward slope toward Silver Creek. *Cory Brockway had found an easier climb to Silver Spring*, Robby thought, *and what he figured to be the roadway leading up to the ancient city*. This had to be what he had found. Now, there was no sign of a road other than the absence of large trees in a pattern that could suggest its path. He also noticed another pattern of trees—willows—that seemed unusually out of place on a hillside. More verdant than the surrounding trees, the line meandered down the hill and continued across a narrow flat to the bank of Silver Creek. Robby decided to check it out.

"Wanna come with me to explore the hill out back?" he called out to Kevin. He didn't see Kevin, but he heard the response.

"No... I'm gonna keep looking for old coins... I found another one."

Robby exited the back door and walked toward the area where he had seen the beginning of the willows, looking casually in all directions as if admiring the view, but in reality searching for eyes. A few minutes later he slid down an embankment to a small stream. Although narrow and shallow, it rippled and gurgled briskly over stones, descending rapidly down the slope. A little farther up the hill, Robby discovered the source: a spring-fed pool no more than three feet wide contained among moss-covered boulders spilled out into another pool, and another, and another, forming the little stream in stair step fashion down the hill. It was completely shaded from the sunlight by the drooping branches of the willows, so no grass grew on the trail alongside, soft with decades of humus and fallen leaves. He found it an engagingly private place and he wondered if Cory had ever discovered this tranquil spot. Probably not. He couldn't recall reading about it anywhere in Cory's journal. Ambling along the trail, frequently ducking low branches, Robby occasionally caught a glimpse of the Lodge, looming largely among the maples and oaks on the hilltop.

Except for the babbling water in the stream, it was hauntingly quiet, the moist, soft earth muffling his footsteps. He paused in a small clearing to marvel at the picturesque scene, and as he stood there, he heard the whirring of the helicopter overhead. And then he heard another noise—the crackling of underbrush off in the distance away from the hill. At first, it bristled the hair on his arms and sent an icy chill down his back. The noise had come from the wrong direction to be made by Kevin, Grant, or Keith. But then he thought it might only be a deer or a coyote. When he could no longer hear the helicopter, Robby was almost back to Tanglewood. Kevin waited on the front verandah.

"Find any more coins?"

"No, just these two," Kevin said. He held them out on an open palm. "This quarter was stuck in a crack in the floor. I had to borrow Punky's knife to dig it out."

Robby picked it out of Kevin's hand and looked for the date: 1896—another coin that had not been in circulation for over a century and in very good condition. "These are quite a find," he told Kevin. "What are you gonna do with 'em?"

"Don't know. Think they're worth a lot?"

"Hard to say... depends on how rare they are."

"How can I find out?"

"You can look them up in coin collecting books at the library."

"Will you help me?"

"Sure... now let's go see what Grant and Punky are doing."

It would have been against all boy rules to leave this place without one more dip in the swimming hole on such a hot day. With the camp all disassembled and packed away in the Jeep, ready for travel, there was nothing pressing to draw them away. Grant felt confident that they had taken a good set of photos. Kevin was excited about his treasure find. Robby and Keith sensed freedom from extra eyes watching them.

Late afternoon, they decided to head for home before the sun went down; finding their way on the trail might not be so easy in the dark.

TWENTY-SIX

"**How was the play?**" Robby asked at the breakfast table. He had been in bed sleeping by the time Phyllis and John came home.

"It was wonderful," Phyllis sighed.

"Your mother would say the Three Stooges were wonderful if she thought their scripts were written by Shakespeare," John mused.

"Oh, John!" Phyllis said. "You enjoyed it, too, and you know it."

"It was okay," John admitted. "But dinner the night before was better."

"Where'd you eat?" Robby asked.

"While your mother and Karen went browsing through antiques shops Saturday afternoon, Bill and I went to a restaurant pub called *Clancy's*."

Robby almost choked on a mouthful of orange juice.

"It's where we all agreed to meet for dinner, John continued. "The steaks were excellent."

"Karen and I had shrimp scampi," Phyllis added. "Best I've ever eaten."

"Next time I'm in Castleburg, I'll be sure to go there," Robby said with a little sarcasm.

"How was camping?" John asked. "Where'd you go?"

"It was great," Robby replied. "Kinda hot, but we found a really neat swimming hole... out in the Wilderness."

"How did Kevin like it?" Phyllis asked. "He's never been wilderness camping before."

"He *didn't* like it at first," Robby said. "But then I told him about the... swimming hole, and he started liking it okay."

John glanced at his wristwatch. "Oh-my-gosh, it's almost nine," he said. He gulped down the last swallow of coffee, buttoned his shirt collar and cinched up his tie. "Gotta go."

Robby watched his dad leave through the patio door, the shortest route to the garage, thankful that the clock had run out and that Dad had not asked more questions about the weekend camping expedition. Eventually, Robby thought, he would have to reveal the secret destination, especially when the time came to explain where and how he and his buddies acquired eleven 70-pound ingots of pure silver. The pure silver, of course, was pure speculation. But until they had exhausted every effort to locate the treasure that *should* be there at Silver Spring, he would do everything in his power to conceal the mission. John Gladstone had always been a skeptic about Silver Spring and its legend, and Robby was quite certain that he would not approve of the boys' current activities.

Robby's cell phone buzzed in his pocket.

"Hello?"

"Are you awake?"

"No, Grant, I'm sound asleep... of course, I'm awake. What's up?"

"Keith and I are looking over the pictures... got 'em downloaded into my computer."

"How do they look?"

"Great... come over and see for yourself."

"Soon as I finish my breakfast... did you eat breakfast yet?"

"Long time ago... must soon be lunchtime, ain't it?"

Robby was well-accustomed to the constant ribbing about not being an early morning riser; the lunchtime poke at him didn't have much impact. "See you in ten," he told Grant and snapped his phone shut. He finished the oatmeal and toast, poured another glass of orange juice and gulped it down. "Thanks for breakfast, Mom. I'll be over at Grant's," he said as he dashed out the back door.

Grant's bedroom resembled the tactical planning arena at the Pentagon. He had already inserted on each picture its number in white, to indicate its place in the sequence, and had weeded out the unnecessary shots due to excessive overlap. A few were a little blurred, but for the most part, they offered all the detail Robby was hoping they would. The stone foundation outlines appeared clearly in all the shots except a few where trees interfered, and some were completely void of any foundation stones, but there was enough to distinguish the streets and the general layout of the old town.

"I'm gonna resize and crop all these to fit together in one file," Grant told Robby. "It'll be easier to work with."

"Better make a copy of those before you start cropping," Robby protested, in fear of accidently losing some valuable information.

"Already did," Grant informed him, and held up a disc.

Three hours later, with Robby and Keith looking over his shoulders, Grant set in place the last of the aerial photos, each one trimmed perfectly to match the edge of the next. They now had the plat of the entire town and the hillsides bordering it; where trees didn't hide it completely, the old railroad tracks were just barely distinguishable on the west side, ruins of the smelter furnaces on the south end, the old hotel near the north end, and at the foot of steep hills and cliffs to the east was a dome tent, fire ring, and a blue Jeep.

"What's that?" Kevin asked. The door was open and he had wandered in.

"The start of our map," Robby quickly told him before Grant had a chance to bark. "These are the pictures Grant took from the helicopter."

"Cool," Kevin replied. "Grant. I'm hungry. When are we gonna eat?"

"We're all hungry," his brother answered. "We'll get some lunch in a little while."

Robby took Kevin aside. "Give us a little while to print out our

94

map, and then we'll all go down to Abbey's for lunch, okay?"

"If we split this into about four sections," Grant advised, "Each section should print on three regular sheets of paper. We might lose some detail if we make it any smaller."

"Then let's do it," Robby said.

A short while later, Robby and Keith started trimming edges and taping the sections together while Grant finished the rest of the printing. Complete, it was a monstrous single unit, but the boys looked upon it as a masterpiece. Now it was a matter of studying Clancy's journal and identifying the streets and buildings. Soon they would know where Oliver went with the silver bars.

"Okay," Robby announced when the map was finished and folded. "Let's go to Abbey's."

They all headed for the black Grand Prix.

TWENTY-SEVEN

Abbey's Café, as usual, was busy during the noon lunch hour. A young, attractive waitress who seemed to know the three recent graduates seated them at a table across the room from the big old clock. When she returned with their beverages, she asked Keith, "Heard from your sister lately?"

"Which one?" Keith replied.

"Eileen... we were in the same class. I haven't seen her since graduation two years ago."

Keith had grown up with two older sisters: Julie had been married for a couple of years and lived in California now, and Eileen was in New York working and going to acting school. Not that he disliked his siblings, he was just thankful when they were both out of the house.   Now it was easier for him to be a guy, and the bathroom was much more accessible.

"No, I haven't heard from Eileen ... but I'm sure Mom has," Keith said. "She's in New York, you know."

"Yes, I knew she was accepted at a college there. Do you have her phone number?"

"Not with me... call my mom... she'll give it to you."

The boys ordered their favorite—Ranch Burgers and Curly Fries. All the while they ate, Robby noticed Keith's occasional curious expressions. Then Kevin said, "What are you gonna do with the map now that you got it printed?"

"It's not finished yet," Robby stated.

"What's left to do with it?"

"We have to figure out the street names."

"How are you gonna do that?"

"With that old diary I told you about."

"Why do you wanna know the street names?"

"'Cause we're—"

"Kevin!" Grant interrupted. "Quit asking so many questions."

With his back to the wall, Keith had a full view of the entire dining area. His brief glance across the room quickly returned to Grant and Robby. In a low voice he asked, "Do either of you know that guy sitting alone at the table just to the right of the clock?"

Robby turned his attention briefly to the lone diner, a middle-aged man in average casual Western attire and in need of a shave. "Nope... never saw him before."

Grant discretely turned to look. "Me either. *Should* we know him?"

"I've seen him in here before," Keith said. "He came in right behind us and he keeps staring over this way."

Both Robby and Grant gave another fleeting look in the man's direction; still a stranger to them, he noticed their attention, apparently embarrassed. He wiped his mouth with a napkin and stood up as if to leave.

"He's just some guy here for lunch," Robby said. "Don't worry 'bout it."

Kevin showed no concern for the stranger. He patted Robby's arm. "Will you go with me to the library?"

"Sure, Kev. When we're done eating."

Keith stared curiously. "What's at the library?"

"Books?" Robby replied jokingly.

"I mean... what are you gonna do there?"

"Look up the old coins Kev found."

"Think they're worth anything?"

"Maybe. We'll find out."

Even though they were interested in learning about Kevin's coins, Grant and Keith displayed little interest in visiting the Public Library right then. They decided, instead, to visit the T-shirt store while Robby accompanied Kevin.

Robby had spent a lot of time at the library during his school years; he was quite familiar with the arrangement, so finding the reference material was only second nature. With relative ease he located a group of books on the subject of coin collecting. He pulled out one entitled Old U.S. Coins, pointed Kevin to a reading table and they sat down. He opened the book, found the section on silver dollars, scanned the material, and then asked Kevin, "What was the date on the silver dollar?"

"Eighteen-ninety-three."

Robby ran his index finger down the chart until he came to the line with the correct year. His lower jaw dropped. "Do you remember the letter by the year?"

"What do you mean?" Kevin said.

"Next to the date... either an S or an O... do you remember?"

"No," Kevin said, "but I have them right here in my pocket." He dug them out.

"You shouldn't be carrying these around in your pocket," Robby scolded. He picked the silver dollar from   Kevin's hand and looked closely for the mint marking. It was an S.

"Holy Christopher Columbus," he mumbled.

"What?" Kevin said. "What does the S mean?"

"The S is for San Francisco Mint, and it means you are *rich!*" Robby held the coin to the page in the book to compare its condition to the grading samples shown; it was every bit as good or better than the "Extra Fine" rating.

Kevin closely inspected the comparison, too. "So, how much does it say it's worth?"

"This coin is worth..." Robby looked around the room to see if anyone else was eavesdropping, and then he lowered his voice to a whisper. "It's worth over five thousand dollars."

Kevin's eyes were bigger than the silver dollar. He started to repeat the figure much too loudly when Robby covered the coin with one hand and Kevin's mouth with the other.

"Shhhhhh," he commanded. "Now, let's see the quarter."

Kevin handed over the other coin. Robby looked for the date

and the mint letter; it, too, was an S, 1896. The quarter was in better condition than the silver dollar.

"San Francisco?" Kevin said.

Robby nodded and turned to the section on quarters. His finger quickly, nervously moved down the chart. He could barely believe his eyes. Kevin had dug out of a crack in the floor a quarter that was worth over thirty-five hundred dollars!

He showed Kevin the line on the chart and then put his finger across his lips. "Don't say anything," he said. "Let's get outa here."

Robby shelved the book and they left.

When they met up with Grant and Keith on the sidewalk, Robby articulated each word as he said to Grant, "Perhaps you should be a little nicer to your brother from now on."

"Why?" Grant's eyes narrowed to just slits.

"Those coins he found out at Silver Spring..."

"Yeah? What? They worth 'bout twelve bucks?"

Robby snickered. "Together they're worth about eighty-five hundred."

"Yeah, right," Grant said.

"Go to the library and look for yourself if you don't believe me."

"Are you serious?" Keith said, amazed.

Kevin just stared blankly at Grant's shoes, his fist firmly wrapped around the coins in his pocket.

TWENTY-EIGHT

"**It just don't seem fair,**" Grant whined after he, Robby, and Keith were alone in his room with the map. "We've put all the work into this and then my little brother waltzes in and snags eighty-five hundred dollars worth of old coins without even trying."

"Why ain't it fair?" Robby questioned. "We all had the same opportunity to pick up that silver dollar out of the dust, and he *did* have to dig that quarter out of a crack in the floor. He *did* put some effort into it."

"Robby's right," Keith defended. "Kev was just lucky on the first one, maybe, but he did take the initiative to *look for more*. We can't hold that against him."

"And besides," Robby added. "When we find the *real* treasure, it's gonna be worth a lot more than that."

"What if you're wrong about all this? You'll be so disappointed."

"Then I'll know I tried. I won't die an old man wondering *what if?* I won't have to regret what I didn't do. I think that's important sometimes."

"What we've gained already has been worth it," Keith said.

"Like what?"

"Like the neat place we've discovered... we can have it all to ourselves 'cause no one else wants to bother with it. We can do whatever we want. Just think of the possibilities. And tell me, Grant... have you found any better place to go skinny dippin' lately?"

"No..."

"And that old hotel... we could clean it up a little... what a great place to spend weekends."

"But the place is haunted."

"So what? We'll make friends with the ghosts."

Robby chimed in, "What Kev found just proves that there's prob'ly lots more to find out there. We've barely just scratched the surface."

"I s'pose you're right," Grant finally conceded.

"Great. Now, let's get to this map... and figure out where Oliver took those silver bars."

He opened Clancy's journal to one of the pages he had flagged, reading aloud from the page: "Julian's Hardware Store is at the corner of Main and Market, right next to the tiny Stationery Store..."

"Clancy mentions the Market Square quite a bit, where the farmers held an open-air market selling produce and stuff right out of their wagons." Keith offered. "It would be my guess that Market Street is the one that crosses Main, here." He pointed to the center of the map. "This short street goes right back to this big area where there aren't any foundations... that must be the Market Square."

"But there isn't any tiny building at that corner," Grant said.

Robby studied the map a moment. The street that Keith had pointed out didn't cross Main, but simply formed a T intersection. "On the other side of Main, though," he said, "this space between these two large buildings is where a tiny store could be... there just isn't a stone foundation."

Grant looked again. "You're prob'ly right. That space isn't wide enough for the street."

"And back here on the square is the livery barn and the

Harness Shop right next to it," Keith said.

Robby referred to the journal again. "This long, narrow building on Main is the Boot and Shoe Repair Shop, and across the street is the Opera House..."

Within a couple of hours they had identified and located on the map many of the business places on Main Street: Julian's Hardware, the Stationery store, the bank, three general stores, two haberdasheries, Hayden and Smith Mining Company offices, drug store, the Continental Billiard Parlor, two other hotels, the Opera House, Tom's Boot & Shoe Repair, restaurants, and more; around the perimeter of the Market Square was a gunsmith, a bakery, a meat market, feed and tack shop, and a green grocer. On other side streets were dress makers, book store, newspaper office, brewery, school and churches.

At suppertime, there were still a lot of unnamed streets and unidentified buildings on the map, but Mrs. B had meatballs, mashed potatoes and gravy waiting.

TWENTY-NINE

Earl and Judy Kraemer were expected to return from their vacation trip any day. Post cards to their neighbors had indicated an enjoyable stay in Seattle, and everyone knew that they weren't the kind of people to bore their friends with endless dull chatter about their daily vacation itinerary and slide shows of them feeding sea gulls and riding ferryboats. So their return was anticipated with eagerness.

The boys thought they should make the homecoming pleasant; Robby mowed the grass while Kevin vacuumed the carpets in the entire house. Grant and Keith cleaned the kitchen and dusted and polished all the furniture. It was the least they could do in appreciation for the anticipated souvenir gifts. Last year they had all received T-shirts from Key West, Florida that they cherished and wore so often that the screen printing was nearly faded away from such frequent laundering. Replacements would be greatly appreciated.

Phyllis Gladstone and Karen Bradley got in on the act, too; Phyllis made Earl's favorite apple pie and Karen baked a huge batch of snicker doodle cookies, both of which were waiting on the kitchen table when the Kraemers pulled in the driveway later that afternoon.

Because no one knew for sure when they would arrive, there was no welcoming party to greet the Kraemers. Grant, Robby, and Keith continued an afternoon cruise around town in the air conditioned comfort of the Grand Prix after they had dropped Kevin off at the park for a soccer game with his friends; Phyllis Gladstone and Karen Bradley enjoyed cold drinks and Gin Rummy on the shaded Bradley front porch; John Gladstone or Bill Bradley wouldn't be home from their daily routines for another couple of hours.

Earl immediately noticed the freshly-groomed lawn; both the Jeep and the Mustang were parked at the curb in front of the Gladstone yard where they weren't subject to flying debris from the mower, so he figured the lawn work had just been completed. He was pleased.

Judy's lower jaw hung like a porch swing when she entered the house through the patio door into the kitchen. She had expected to spend a day cleaning and washing dishes in the wake of two teen-agers alone in the house for nearly three weeks. But instead, she and Earl could sit down and relax, and enjoy some coffee and fresh snicker doodle cookies—in a very tidy house.

Compulsively driven, Judy called the Gladstone residence. No answer. Karen Bradley, though, answered on the fourth ring. "We're home," Judy announced.

"Welcome home!" Karen replied. *"How was your trip?"*

"We took our time from Seattle… spent one of the nights in Essex at the *Izaak Walton Inn*… what a wonderful place… I'm assuming the cookies and pie came from you and Phyllis? Thank you, so much."

"You're quite welcome. Phyllis and I are having iced tea… would you and Earl care to join us?"

"Sure, I will," Judy said. "But Earl is already in his office at the computer… probably catching up on all the e-mails that have piled up. Grant's Jeep is here but he *or* Kevin are nowhere in sight. There was no answer next door. Are the boys at your house?"

"No… they're all off somewhere in Keith's car. I think Kevin is playing soccer at the park."

After all the welcome home greetings and hugs—moms are required to hug everybody after an extended absence—Judy announced that Earl had agreed to grill hamburgers for anyone who was interested. There were no objections. She handed Grant a twenty-dollar bill and sent him to *Hy-Vee* to pick up four pounds of ground beef. "And then go to the bakery," she instructed. "Get two dozen of those really good hamburger buns."

While Grant was gone on the grocery run, Robby and Keith went to their respective homes and helped their moms gather a few goodies to supply the cookout.

Kevin tried hard not to be a pest to his dad, but he had so much news to share. "Dad! Dad!" he bubbled as he entered Earl's office. "I went with Grant and Robby and Punky camping last weekend…"

"How was the Soccer Training Camp?" Earl asked, recognizing Kevin's excitement but somewhat ignoring it, accustomed to his over-exuberance at times. He continued to stare at his computer screen.

"It was great… but let me tell you about our camping trip first."

"Okay, son. What was so special about your camping trip?"

"We went out in the wilderness and Robby took me to an old abandoned hotel where there used to be a town that burned down long time ago. He said it was haunted but we never saw any ghosts or anything. Yeah, and when we were lookin' around in that old hotel I found a couple of real old coins… a silver dollar and a quarter. Guess how much they're worth."

"I don't know," Earl replied. "I haven't seen them. How much?"

"Eight thousand five hundred dollars."

That got Earl's attention. "How do you know?"

"Robby took me to the library the next day and he looked it up in a book."

"Where are the coins now?" Earl asked, his full attention now focused on his ecstatic young son.

"I hid 'em in my sock drawer."

"Get them for me… let's look them up on the internet." Earl seemed a little skeptical.

Kevin raced up the stairs to his room, and a minute later he returned to his dad's office holding the shiny silver coins in his open palm. Earl took them, turned them over several times inspecting them, impressed with their excellent condition, and then laid them on his desk under the light. He typed in a website search, and within just a few seconds he had a chart on the screen that listed vintage silver dollar values. He examined the one on his desk for the mint identification letter. "Eighteen-ninety-three, San Francisco mint," he said aloud and then returned his astonished stare back to the screen. His reaction duplicated when he had identified the 1896 San Francisco quarter's value.

"And where did you say you found these? In an abandoned building?" he asked.

"Yeah... out in the wilderness... where we went camping."

"Isn't that the place that I've heard the stories about some local legend? That it's haunted?"

"Yeah, that's what Robby told me. But we were there the *whole* weekend and I didn't see a *single* ghost... and we found this really neat place to go swimming, too."

"Well, you found yourself quite a treasure, here, Kev. We'd better find a better place than your sock drawer to keep them."

"Where are you gonna put 'em? Can't I sell 'em and get my money?"

"Kev... coins that valuable won't be easy to sell... not for that much. It could take months... years to find a buyer willing to spend that much."

Kevin's face turned a little sour. "So... where should I keep 'em?"

"I'll put them in my safe for now."

"Do we hafta? I won't ever be able to look at 'em."

"Yes, Kev... it's the safest thing to do, so they don't get lost or stolen. I'll open the safe so you can see them any time you want."

THIRTY

With the coins tucked safely behind a combination lock, each coin in a separate envelope so they wouldn't rub together, Earl and Kevin went to the back yard to start the gas grill. In a little while, the aroma of sizzling hamburgers seemed to draw a friendly, hungry crowd. John Gladstone and Bill Bradley were glad to have their neighbors home again, and the moms were delighted to once again participate in a joint effort to feed the whole gang.

"I was beginning to wonder if you were gonna stay in Seattle for the Fourth of July," John kidded. "Our Fourth Barbeque just wouldn't be the same."

It didn't necessarily take a special occasion or holiday for a Gladstone/Bradley/Kraemer barbeque get-together, but the Fourth of July was when they invited other neighbors, friends and family to join them, as well. It wasn't unusual to see thirty or forty people amassed in their back yards with at least three grills smoking up the whole neighborhood.

"Oh, heavens, no," Earl exclaimed, flipping burgers on the grill. "We couldn't miss that!"

Grant waited for an opportune moment after everyone had eaten to discretely talk with his dad.

"Did Kevin tell you about the coins?" he asked.

"Yes, he did," Earl responded. "They're in my safe now."

"Good. Did he tell you where he found them?"

"Yes, he told me all about it."

"Please don't say anything about any of this to John. Robby doesn't want him to know we were out there yet."

"Why?"

"He just doesn't... that's all. John's kinda touchy about it, I guess. Oh... and by the way... I used the remote digital for some aerial photos from the helicopter out there."

Earl eyed his son suspiciously, but then conceded to Grant's good judgment. "How'd it work?"

"Great!" Grant grinned.

Before the outdoor dinner party had ended, Judy retrieved a package from the house.

"Because the Key West T-shirts were such a hit last year," she said, "We decided on the same this year." She opened the package and started pulling out various colored shirts with a picture of the Space Needle and the name *Seattle* screen-printed across the front. "White for Keith, because he likes white T-shirts; yellow for Robby because he has a yellow convertible; blue for Grant because he has a blue Jeep; and red for Kevin... because we don't know *what* he is yet."

The boys all slipped off the T-shirts they were wearing and pulled on the new ones. They stood together; "Thanks, Mom!" they sang out in unison, and then they all offered an individual 'thank you' to Earl as well. Moms and Dads admired the four handsome lads in their new shirts, and Phyllis clicked a snapshot.

"Didn't you just recently do some electronics work for the Space Needle?" Bill asked Earl.

"I was just their consultant," Earl replied. "I advised the designers on some of the electronics for the new information kiosks on the observation deck. Judy and I got to see them in action."

"Were you satisfied?" John asked.

"Very much so. They did an outstanding job."

The men rarely discussed their work during social gatherings like this unless it seemed appropriate. Earl wasn't actually discussing his work, but rather, he was describing the result of his work—the communication and information system used at an attraction that interested both John and Bill.

"I was at a bank conference in Seattle once," John said. "But I never had time to visit the Needle."

"You should do it sometime," Earl replied. "I think you'd

really enjoy it."

"It'll have to be next year," John said. "Phyllis and I have hotel reservations for a week at Catalina Island in September... how 'bout you, Bill? Where are you and Karen going this year?"

"Our daughter, Julie, and her husband want us to come to San Francisco; we'll probably go for a week in August."

While the dads talked about vacation spots and the moms got Judy caught up on the neighborhood gossip, the boys engaged in two-on-two basketball. It was Grant's turn for first choice of a teammate; he chose his brother.

THIRTY-ONE

"Hey, Rumpelstiltskin! You gonna wake up sometime in this decade?"

Robby heard Grant's familiar voice; he opened one eye and squinted at his bedside clock—8:40. "Rumpel-who?" he said with a scratchy voice.

"The guy who slept for twenty years," Grant replied, laughing.

"No," Robby heard Keith say. "That was Rip Van Winkle. Rumpelstiltskin spun straw into gold."

"Yeah," Robby growled. "Get your fairy tales straight."

"Well, whoever it was. Day's wastin'… time to get *your* fairy tale out of bed."

Robby sat on the edge of the bed; Grant and Keith sat beside him. "We've been thinking," Grant said, "that if we finish figuring out that map this morning, maybe we'd have time to go out to Silver Spring this afternoon and look around some more… with the map."

"Okay… but I promised Dad I'd mow *our* lawn today."

By the time Robby ate breakfast and rolled out the Lawn-Boy, Grant had the Kraemer's mower at work in the front lawn, and Keith had the trimmer in action along the fence and around the garden. The entire lawn, including the trimming was finished in a fraction of the time it normally took Robby.

"Why didn't you just work on the map?" Robby asked as the Lawn-Boy found its dark corner in the garage.

"There's too many people hangin' around our house," Grant said.

"And Mrs. B is on a cleaning frenzy at our house," said Keith.

"Well, I don't want my mom zeroing in on what we're doing,"

Robby complained. "She's already asked me about the old journal... I think she knows where it came from."

"Okay," said Grant. "Then let's go down to Abbey's."

"Thought you didn't want a lot of people hangin' around," Robby said. There'll be a crowd there this time of day."

"Where, then?"

"The library," Robby said confidently. "They have bigger tables to spread out the map, and there shouldn't be so many people. And it's not so far to Abbey's from there... we can have lunch when we get hungry."

The Mustang with the top down was voted the carriage of the day. The library proved quiet and private—a few, but not many people were confining themselves on such a pleasant day.

After a couple of hours with the map spread out on one of the big tables, they had written a name or some notation on nearly every building foundation showing, and had even identified some of the spaces where there were no foundations at all, assuming that some structures in those early times may have been built without them. Most of the streets had names, now, too.

Keith stood back and admired their work. "Should be easy to follow Oliver's path now," he said.

Robby had bookmarked all the places in the journal where Clancy had described his sightings of Oliver's early morning walks toting the heavily-laden burlap bag over his shoulder. As he read the passages aloud, Keith and Grant located the place and penciled in an arrow indicating direction of Oliver's travel. All indications, so far, revealed a north and west movement.

"Okay," Grant said. "He must've been going somewhere in the northwest corner of town." He pointed to the area between Tanglewood Lodge and the railroad depot.

It made sense according to all the arrows on the map. They studied that corner of town. There wasn't much there except a barber shop, a doctor's office, dressmaker shop, and according to Clancy, a 'dumpy' little saloon.

Keith had an idea: "All the saloons had a cellar to keep the beer cold," he said. "Oliver could've slipped the ingots into a cellar."

"Not that one," Robby argued. "Clancy also said the *Pickaxe Saloon* had the warmest beer in town. Don't think it had a cellar."

"Well, then, what other places had a cellar?"

"Only the hotels and saloons... and a couple of the General Stores, but most of them are downtown or on the other end of town."

"Besides," Grant added. "When Oliver was swiping the silver, all the businesses like that were still operating in full swing. I don't think he'd hide them in any of those places... too many chances of it being found."

They all agreed that Oliver hadn't stowed the silver ingots in a beer cellar. They studied the map some more.

"Maybe Oliver had a girlfriend," Grant said. "The dressmaker?"

"He was a loner... remember?"

"Oh, yeah... no girlfriend."

"It must be in this part of town, somewhere," Keith said. "I think we should just go out there and search closely... maybe take some shovels along in case we need to dig. We've still got all afternoon."

"Okay," Robby said. "But let's go to Abbey's first... I'm hungry."

THIRTY-TWO

The cooler ride through the forested hills and prairie grass valleys came to an abrupt halt when the boys found themselves under a baking sun on the hilltop that had once been Silver Spring. Almost immediately Keith stripped off his shirt. His tanned, muscled arms and shoulders glistened with sweat. It wasn't long before Grant and Robby followed his lead; shirtless, toting shovels they borrowed from the Gladstone garden shed, Robby with a backpack strapped over one shoulder, they plodded toward the northwest knoll, where the terrain dropped down an easy grade to the prior site of the railroad station.

Robby unfurled the map that he pulled from the backpack, stood so the map lined up, corresponding to the visible rock foundations. They identified the doctor's office, barber shop, dressmaker shop, and the Pickaxe Saloon, the last building down the slope before a large open space separated it from the railroad tracks. Clancy had described a large warehouse with nothing more than a dirt floor at that location. So far, his narrative description of the town had proven quite accurate.

Hearts pounding with excitement, having narrowed the search to a much smaller area, they lined up abreast of each other about six feet apart and began walking slowly, eyes fixed to the ground, picking, probing, and scrutinizing every rock big enough to cast a shadow. Working their way from the first foundation stones next to the hotel toward the railroad tracks, along the rear of the long-gone buildings, nothing revealed itself as noteworthy. On the return sweep closer to the street side of the foundations, however, Grant, who was closest to the street, probed the tip of his shovel into the ground; the unmistakable metallic ring caught Robby's and Keith's attention as well. Clustered together, shoulder-to-shoulder, they watched as Grant's shovel cleared the grass and weeds and then scratched through the thin layer of gravel and clay. Something metallic lay just beneath the surface.

Little by little, the object was unearthed, and although they were not totally disappointed with their find, they were well aware that it wasn't the treasure they sought. When the dirt was brushed away, they were grasping a cast-iron horse's head with a large ring through its nose.

"What is it?" Grant said curiously.

Robby studied the object a moment. "A hitching post," he said. With his fingers he dug the dirt from the hollowed out horse's neck. "This would fit over the top of a wooden post," he explained, and then pointing to the ring, "This is where a horse's reigns were tied so they wouldn't wander off while the rider... was in a store... or somewhere..."

He and Keith suddenly looked away from the artifact, flitting inquisitive glances in various directions.

"What's the matter with you guys?" Grant questioned.

"Don't know," Robby said. "It just felt like..."

"Like what?" Grant said.

Keith said with a mysterious tone of voice: "Like someone was watching us?"

"Yeah... sort of..." Robby said.

"You guys are crazy," Grant scolded. "There ain't nobody but us... anywhere around."

"Yeah, you're prob'ly right," Keith conceded.

They continued the search back to the hotel, finding only the mate to the first hitching post head. After combing the steeper upward slope behind the row of foundations, they returned, somewhat dejected, to the intersection of Main and Connor Streets in front of Tanglewood Lodge.

Robby pulled out the map again and unfolded it; something

seemed to bother him. He pondered a few moments, gazed off to the south, to the east, and then back to the map again. "Wait a minute," he said. "Something's not right."

"What?" Keith asked.

With a purposeful stride, Robby started walking southward through the tall grass. "I wanna find the intersection of Main and Market... I think we made a mistake."

Grant and Keith didn't question Robby's remark. They both knew that he had studied the journals more thoroughly, and now it seemed that he was giving thoughtful consideration to a possible error in their cartography.

Keith remembered while flying the helicopter for the photos, stumbling over some of the foundations, and then encountering a large open area clear of any obstructions. He returned to that place, and then found the wide passage between two large buildings that led back to Main Street.

"That's the market square," he said pointing, "And this must be Market Street."

Robby agreed with his logic. He studied the map again, and then paced across what he believed to be Main until he reached another stone foundation hiding in the weeds. Locating the corner, he paced again northward to the next stones. He put the map down and started digging among the tall grass. "Come here and help me," he beckoned to Keith and Grant.

"What are we digging here for?" Keith asked.

"You'll see," Robby replied, sweat dripping from his chin. "Spread out, and dig down only about six or eight inches in several spots."

Grant and Keith complied with his instructions. When they had uncovered nothing but small stones and shale evenly distributed over the area, Robby then consulted the map.

"Okay," he said, and paced diagonally across Main again to another foundation. Just inside its perimeter he started poking the tip of the shovel into the ground in arbitrary pattern. Grant and Keith watched. "Do what I'm doing..." he told them. "All over inside this one."

"What are we looking for here?" Grant asked. "More rocks?"

"No. Anything metal," Robby said.

In a short time, Keith struck something that wasn't just stones. Robby came to inspect. Pawing in the dirt that Keith had loosened with the shovel, he found what appeared to be a large heap of carpenter's nails, rusted and nearly diminished to nothing, but still distinguishable as nails.

Robby smiled. "This proves it," he said.

"What? Proves what?" Keith asked.

"Over there," Robby started to explain. "Where we found nothing but gravel just under the surface, there was no building... that material is what would be used to pave a street... or an alley."

"Okay," Keith said, agreeing with Robby's assumption. "What about this?" he said pointing to the rusty nails.

"A hardware store," Robby beamed. "This is probably the remains of a nail keg left behind. Why else would there be a large quantity of nails in a downtown store?"

Grant and Keith agreed, but they were still confused with Robby's reasoning, even though it made sense.

"It occurred to me when I remembered Clancy writing that *Oliver came down the narrow alley by Julian's Hardware Store, crossed the street and then headed toward Tom's."*

"Yeah?" Grant said. "That meant he was going in that direction." He pointed north.

"Wrong," Robby said. "We had the hardware store on the wrong side of the street." He retrieved his backpack and dug out the journal. While he frantically paged through Clancy's poor penmanship, Keith stared at the map. "But the tiny shop next to it—"

"That's what I'm looking for now," Robby interrupted. "Where we were digging first *was* an alley, but we had it as the *tiny* stationery store." He flipped a few more pages. "Aha! Here it is! "That's not a *tiny* store... the guy who owned it was *called*

Tiny... a fat man named Tiny, Clancy says. That's his store where we don't have a name written in."

"But if he headed toward Tom's, meaning Tom's Boot Repair, he was *still* going north up Main Street," Grant disputed.

"No," Robby disagreed again. "Clancy just wrote *Tom's,* not *Tom's Boot Repair.* One of Clancy's best friends in Silver Spring was *Tom* Hargrove, the newspaper reporter. *Tom* lived close to the newspaper office and printing shop, so whether Clancy meant *Tom's house* or *Tom's office,* both of which are east of Main Street, it puts him heading toward the *east* side of town, right through *that alley."* Robby pointed to where they dug up small stones and shale. "It also means that all the places we marked on the map, using the hardware store and the *tiny* store as reference points, we've got it all wrong. We have to start over."

The sun was getting low over the western horizon, painting the clouds in brilliant reds, pinks, and grays. There would be just enough time to cross the hills toward Wellington before dark.

THIRTY-THREE

They were too late for supper, but they really didn't mind; pizza and Cokes down in the Kraemer man cave seemed the perfect way to finish off the day. They had made great progress, even if the progress meant fixing an earlier mistake. At least now their map would be more accurate and helpful.

The next morning after Robby had been rousted out of bed and had run some downtown errands for Mrs. G, the boys went back to work in earnest on their map. Robby was determined to get every detail as precise as possible, and to make sure he didn't overlook any more little elements that might prevent them from another senseless scavenger hunt for rusty cast-iron horse's heads. Grant printed another set of the aerial photos so they had a clean copy of the map to work with, and when they had relabeled the store names they knew to be incorrect on the first map, they carefully proceeded to identify the rest of the buildings with a little less haste. Even though Clancy had provided a good description—although brief—he had neglected the use of compass points for direction, and distances were also quite vague. But with a correct start and reference point, more of the buildings had names and their orientation seemed more logical.

When they retraced Oliver's movements on the new map from Clancy's narrative log, now his paths pointed to the northeast corner of the town. This made more sense because there were more features of urban development for a greater distance in that direction, and far more opportunities for a treasure to be concealed.

Another outing to Silver Spring was planned: they would leave early the next morning so they would have the entire day— their last available day before the big Fourth of July barbeque. A cooler was stocked with an ample supply of hot dogs and Cokes and another shopping bag was filled with cookies and potato chips and hot dog buns—plenty to keep them sustained for a day.

"Hey, Kev," Grant said discretely to his little brother that evening. "We're goin' out to our secret place again tomorrow... wanna go along? You can hunt for more coins."

Kevin gave it a moment of thought. "Are you camping out overnight? We have a Summer League soccer game on Saturday."

"No, we're not camping overnight... just goin' early in the morning and coming back tomorrow afternoon."

"Can we go swimming?"

"Sure... we can go swimming for a while, too."

"Okay... I'll go. What time are we leaving?"

"If Robby gets his butt outa bed, about nine o'clock."

"That's not early."

"It is for Robby."

THIRTY-FOUR

The *early* morning departure was more of a shock to his mother, especially when Robby was up at seven a.m. and informed her that he would be having breakfast at Grant's house.

"Just remember," John Gladstone reminded his son. "We have to get the yard ready for the barbeque on Sunday... it's the Fourth, you know."

"I'll be here to work on it all day tomorrow," Robby replied. "How many people are coming this year?" he asked, trying to keep the conversation steered away from the reason for his leaving so early.

"Don't know... the usual open invitation is out there for anyone who wants to come."

"Being a Sunday," Phyllis added, "We might get a bigger crowd."

"Well, I'm sure it will be a lot of fun as usual," Robby said. "Grant and Keith and I are going down to the river early Sunday night... so we can get a good spot to watch the fireworks." With that he was out the back, headed to the Kraemer's house next door. He had disappeared through the gate in the tall wooden privacy fence before it dawned on John to ask any more questions about the boys' activities starting so early that day.

Judy and Earl Kraemer had finished an early breakfast, too, sitting at the table drinking coffee when Robby entered through the patio door, Keith right behind him.

"Grant and Kevin are taking showers," Judy informed them. "They'll be down shortly... so in the meantime, you can sit down and start eating." She uncovered a large platter of steaming scrambled eggs, crispy bacon, and a mountain of buttered toast. A few minutes later, Grant and Kevin joined them, and the four teen-aged vacuum cleaners rid the table of anything edible.

"So, where are you boys off to so early?" Earl asked.

"Um... exploring," Grant offered.

"Out to hunt for some more old coins," Earl said smiling.

"Um... maybe..."

"And swimming!" Kevin added.

"Well, good hunting," Earl said. "But be back here tomorrow to help with the yard work... gotta get it ready for Sunday."

"We'll be back this afternoon," Grant assured his dad.

"Did you get enough to eat?" Judy asked as the boys excused themselves from the table.

"Yes, plenty, Mrs. K," Robby replied.

"It was great, Mrs. K!" Keith added.

"I'm making meatloaf for dinner tonight," Judy announced as they were going out the patio door. "Don't be late!"

The four boy choir sang out, "We won't... thanks, Mom." They were pushovers for her pot roast and cherry cheese-cake, and they might even commit murder for her meatloaf. It was a good reason to be home early.

Their journeys to Silver Spring had worn a visible trail through the wilderness, easy to follow without the need to recall landmarks to aid navigation. The trips seemed shorter now that they were more familiar with the landscape.

"The trail is almost too visible," Robby said. "What if somebody follows us?"

"It's not hunting season," Keith responded. "And besides hunters, no one else is apt to come out here, so no one will even see our tracks."

Robby quietly accepted Keith's theory, hopeful that he was

right. He probably was; no one since Cory Brockway in 1968 had ventured into this territory with such a dark and frightening history, and now, with their profound discovery, perhaps it was a good idea to just go along with the beliefs of a murderous spirit lurking about in these hills, even if they knew it was bogus. He could think of no reason to lure others there—best to just keep everything covert and completely out of sight from any other potential intruders.

A dark forest-green four-wheel-drive Ford half-ton with moderately over-sized off-road tires cruised past the Kraemer and Gladstone houses about 10:15. The driver was one of the older members of the off-road club that Grant had fraternized with a few days nearly a month ago. The truck was the only product of the owner's meager inheritance from his deceased parents. A farm boy at heart, the truck was an important part of his life, but his life in the country had ended years ago. Now, with not many friends left, he clung to a few off-roaders who accepted him for who he was.

Another pass by the Kraemer house, absent of Jeep in the driveway, indicated that Grant Kraemer was not at home. He drove away.

Nothing had changed since their last visit to the Silver Spring plateau. Birds still provided a song in the air, accompanied by the comforting whistle of the breeze in the treetops and the murmuring rush of swift current over the rocks in Silver Creek. The perfume of wildflowers seemed almost intoxicating. It was easy to see why the pioneers had chosen this spot for their town; it was equally difficult to imagine why this utopia had been shunned by its modern-day neighbors.

"Wanna go look for coins in the hotel while we... um... work on our map?" Grant said to Kevin. They had stopped at the intersection of Main and Market Streets.

The younger brother gazed at the old building, and then looked at Robby with pleading eyes.

"You'll be okay alone," Robby said calmly. "Just be careful on the stairs if you wanna go up."

"Where are you guys gonna be?" Kevin asked.

"We'll be close by... right around here in this area," Robby assured him. "We won't be far away. Got your flashlight?"

Kevin nodded and patted his hip pocket.

It was another very hot day; as Kevin hiked off to Tanglewood up Main Street, Keith stripped off his T-shirt. Grant and Robby did the same. If nothing else, they were acquiring tans equal to Keith's, something neither of them had ever accomplished.

THIRTY-FIVE

Sheriff Haley Moore pulled his squad car up to the curb in front of the Kraemer's house. Unlike all the deputy squads, his burgundy *Ford Crown Victoria* sedan lacked any markings or roof lights.   Only the very observant would notice the law enforcement license plates, the multiple fine-wire radio antennas on the trunk lid, and the minuscule placard next to the left taillight declaring: *Wellington County Sheriff.* Most of the time, Haley Moore wore plain clothes—plaid shirts and khakis—in uniform only for parades and election campaigns. He preferred maintaining a low public profile for more effective investigations when the need arose.

Haley pressed the doorbell button and waited.

Earl opened the door. "Well, hello, Haley," Earl greeted the sheriff, and then instinctively thought about his sons. "Is something wrong, Sheriff?"

"Hi, Earl... no, no, nothing's wrong... at least not yet. Just wondering if we could have a little chat."

"What about? Would you like to come in? Have some coffee?"

"Oh, no. But thanks. It'll just take a minute. Right here on the stoop will be just fine."

"What did you want to chat about?"

"Well, it's your boys... Kevin and Grant."

"Are they getting into some kind of trouble?"

"No, not yet."

"What do you mean? Not yet?"

"Well, I got word that your youngest, Kevin, told some of his friends that he'd found some pretty valuable old coins."

"Yes, he did. I have them locked in my safe. Is there a problem with that?"

"The only problem is *where* he found them."

"In an old abandoned building," Earl defended his son.

"Yes," said the sheriff. "Out in the wilderness. Those boys shouldn't really be out there."

"It's public land, is it not?"

"Yes, it's public land... of course..."

"Did they break any laws going there?"

"No," Sheriff Moore said, his frustration mounting. "It's just that... well... you haven't lived in Wellington all your life. You probably don't know about..." He looked around and then whispered, "*Mack.*"

"Yes, Haley, I've read some very entertaining stories about the *legend of Mack*. And that's all it is... *a legend.*"

"I sure wish you'd take this a little more seriously," said the sheriff.

"Look, Sheriff... Haley. We've known each other since I helped you get elected the first time... what? Five, six years ago?"

"Six."

"Well, I'm sorry, Haley, but I can't stand here and let you tell me that my boys can't go on public land to hunt for old coins just because of some foolish folklore. If they're not breaking any laws, then I can't see anything wrong with it. They're *kids*, dammit. Let them be *kids* for Chrissake."

Sheriff Haley Moore knew he couldn't stop the boys from going out into the wilderness; there were no laws prohibiting entry. Hunters used that land every year, but the locals were aware of the boundaries—*they knew not to cross the dead line.*

That legend had lived and cycled since the turn of the last century: it had proven itself justifiable every forty years, or so. And it was almost time for another spectacular installment of *Mack Terrifies Wellington County.* Although the trepidation that Silver Spring created, the image it spawned in the general public's eye was that of splendid ghost tales, their very own *Headless Horseman of Sleepy Hollow.* The mysterious castles of Old England emitting the haunting sounds of clattering chains and grotesque moans of horror from long ago isolated dungeons far below the surface had nothing on Wellington County. A ghastly specter they called Mack, the ghost of a Nineteenth Century desperado had been blamed for many deaths; it was still believed that he was protecting a treasure that the living could only speculate on its actual existence or worth. But despite his horrible reputation, the public somehow loved him and would loathe the thought of him vanishing from their culture. The newsmen, too, loved his sensationalism; his stories of terror sold a lot of newspapers.

"Will you be stopping by on Sunday for our grand July Fourth barbeque?" Earl asked when he noticed Haley seemed quite defeated.

"Oh... sure... I'd love to."

THIRTY-SIX

"First thing we should do is determine the farthest point in this direction where Clancy saw Oliver carrying the full bag," Robby said.

"And then," Keith added. "Are there any basements or cellars in this part of town?"

"Just one possibility that I can see," Robby said as he studied the map. "The Silver Star Saloon. But I thought we decided that Oliver didn't put the silver in a beer cellar."

"Just a thought."

"Looks like he always came from the same place downtown," Grant said.

"Yeah. He lived in a room upstairs at the Continental... right here," Robby said, pointing.

"Clancy saw him on Connor Street... a couple of times," Keith said. "The street farthest north."

"Probably avoiding other people," Robby said. "He also saw him heading down Johnson Street past the bakery toward the newspaper office. That means he was going south from Connor. His final destination wasn't as far north as Connor Street."

"Here he's going east on Flatrock..."

After much careful consideration of Oliver's direction of travel and the general vicinity of his destination, Robby, Grant, and Keith took up their shovels, headed up Main Street, probing the tall grass for foundations, and counting off the buildings and the blocks until they came to the intersection with Flatrock. They turned eastward and continued the same procedure until they came to the very spot that Clancy had proclaimed as the farthest point he had witnessed Oliver toting the full bag of silver. They stood there a few minutes contemplating the odds.

"How could Clancy have seen Oliver in all these different places from Tanglewood... or on his way to the Market Square?" Keith pondered.

"You're right," Grant said. "Too many obstacles in the way."

They had studied that map and imagined the sights of an 1890's Silver Spring so long and so intensely that they almost felt like they were standing on streets with the buildings still looming before them, towering above them, and board sidewalks at their feet. They could almost hear the whinny of horses and wagon wheels clattering along cobblestone streets. They could easily imagine a line of miners with shouldered shovels and pickaxes parading off to some distant mineshaft.

To the boys, Silver Spring had virtually come back to life.

"You know what I think?" Robby said.

"What?"

"I think Clancy must've followed Oliver sometimes. I think he knows where Oliver took the silver ingots."

"Think he got 'em after Oliver was killed?"

"No, he didn't."

"What makes you so sure?"

"He wouldn't have left his brother's wife and daughter all alone. He wouldn't have gotten on that riverboat to work as a simple deckhand. No. He knew where the silver was hidden so safely that nobody would ever find it, and with the whole town totally destroyed and deserted, he thought he'd come back to it someday."

"And then he went off to war and got himself killed," Keith said.

"Well, *we don't know* where Oliver went," Grant said. "So what are our options?"

"Clancy said he always returned in about five minutes with the bag empty."

Grant gazed in all directions. "That's a couple of minutes each way. Two minutes that way is the very edge of town," he said pointing east. "Two minutes that way puts him almost back to Connor Street." He gestured toward the north. "Two minutes that way..." Grant waved southward as if to dismiss the idea. "That doesn't even make any sense. Why would he come all this way north and then go back south?"

"I think the east edge of town is the best bet," said Keith.

It seemed the most logical alternative. They all agreed that all of Clancy's sightings positioned Oliver on a course toward Flatrock Street; somewhere within two or three minutes' walking time had been Oliver's destination.

Robby consulted the map with each building foundation they passed on Flatrock Street: a flower shop; a boarding house; a butcher shop; a small bakery; another boarding house; the Lighthouse.

"The Lighthouse?" Keith questioned.

"Yeah," Robby replied. "It's a store that sold lanterns, candles, and lamp oil."

"Clever name," Grant added.

They continued picking their way along Flat-rock Street until it ended, according to the aerial photo map, at the last street on that side of town, appropriately named East Street. At that corner, Clancy had placed a blacksmith shop and its owner's house. Beyond that were a few trees on a narrow strip of land at the edge of a vertical rock cliff, the valley floor at least a hundred feet below.

"There's nowhere else for him to go," Grant stated as he peered over the edge of the cliff. He was implying that their search should begin in this area.

In the same manner as they had used to search the northwest

corner of town, they began their scrutiny here, starting at Flatrock, first northward along East Street, poking at every square inch within the walls of each building. They had passed over several when that unnerving sensation of being watched nagged at Robby. He looked at the other two; Grant's head was down, his eyes intensely focused on the ground at his feet, but Keith's distant gaze suggested that he was concentrating on something else. His eyes met Robby's, and they didn't have to speak the words. Each knew what the other was thinking.

Just then, Kevin's voice split the serenity like an axe through a block of wood. "ROBBY! ROBBY!" he called out. "I FOUND SOME MORE!"

They temporarily suspended the search as they watched Kevin coming from the old hotel, winding and stumbling his way through a patch of birch trees, the previous site of a carriage house behind an undertaker's parlor. When he finally reached the others, he held out a fistful of tarnished coins.

"These were scattered all over behind the bar," he said with excitement. "A lot of busted glass, too."

Grant and Keith stepped closer to see Kevin's newest discoveries. What appeared to be mostly nickels and   dimes gave Robby more confidence.

"You see?" he said to Grant and Keith. "This is the reason I think no one else has ever been here looking for..." He paused and stared at Kevin, suddenly remembering that Kevin shouldn't know about the big treasure they were searching for.

"Looking for what?" Kevin asked curiously.

"For... for... for historical artifacts," Robby stuttered.

Kevin stared with conceivable doubt. "You're hunting for some kinda treasure, ain't ya?"

There was no point in trying to hide the truth from the perceptive youngster. "Yeah, Kev, we are," Robby said calmly and firmly. "But you have to promise that you won't tell *anybody* about this."

"Why?"

"'Cause we don't want a bunch of other people coming out here looking for it, too. This has to be our secret."

"Why don't people come to look for it anyway?"

"'Cause only we know about it."

"Why doesn't anybody else know?"

"'Cause nobody—ever—knew it was missing."

"Knew *what* was missing?"

"Silver bars... a whole bunch of 'em."

"Where'd they come from?"

"Some guy stole them from the silver smelter; this was a mining town. It's all in that diary I told you about."

"So that's the secrets you know, huh?"

THIRTY-SEVEN

The search of a six block area had uncovered no more than a few rusty horseshoes, a wrought-iron porch railing, and a steel lamp post. In the shade of the trees at the edge of the cliff, they sat for a rest. It was well past lunchtime.

"What are we missing?" Keith mumbled.

Robby extracted Clancy's journal from his backpack, thumbed through several pages. "There's some clue that we've overlooked," he said as he scanned the pages, hoping to spot something that he might have missed.

"Maybe it wasn't five minutes," Grant said. "Maybe it was ten."

"What d'ya mean?" Keith responded.

"Well, Clancy lacked direction and distance in his details... maybe he wasn't too good at time, either. Did you ever notice anywhere in his book that he mentioned having a watch?"

"Good point," Keith said.

Robby pondered on that a few moments and then arrived at the conclusion that Grant might be on to something.

"I'm hungry!" Kevin complained. "Can we eat lunch now?"

"Yeah, I'm hungry, too," Robby agreed. "Let's go roast some weenies."

They hiked back down to their old campsite, rounded up some firewood, ignited a fire, and proceeded to devour a couple of pounds of hot dogs and a large bag of potato chips, washed down with ice-cold Cokes.

The uneasy sentiment of visual violation upon them had not left Keith. In fact, it was stronger now, but rather than causing alarm to the others, he said nothing. *There was no one else there but them*, he thought. *How could there be? Maybe Robby was right... maybe Mack really was keeping tabs on their every move. They had crossed the dead line, and Mack was making sure they didn't wander too close to the treasure.*

Keith shook off the mirage of the bushy black mustache and beard, the dusty black hat, vest, chaps and boots, all worn by the dastardly villain wielding a six-gun and a torch, an image that he had conjured up of a Nineteenth Century bank robber that was known to have set the city of Silver Spring ablaze. But to think that his ghost was following them was simply absurd.

"Let's extend our search a little farther," Robby said as they let the hot dogs settle. "If Grant's theory is correct, Oliver might've gone farther... more than just a couple minutes away."

"Can we go swimming now?" Kevin begged.

"Not now, Kev," Grant answered. "We've got things to do yet... later."

"Well, can I go swimming while you—"

"No, Kev," Robby said. "You can't go swimming *alone* in the creek. It's too dangerous. We'll all go together, later, okay?"

They trekked back up the hillside and resumed the hunt in a wider circle from Flatrock Street. Keith unearthed another hitching post head, Grant uncovered some well-preserved door hinges, and Robby found what appeared to be a cluster of garden tools. Kevin sat in the shade, intrigued with the map, pieced together with aerial pictures.

"What's this?" he asked when the three treasure hunters returned to the shade for a rest.

"A map," his brother blurted out.

"No... this," Kevin said, pointing to the eastern edge of the map.

Grant leaned down to see what Kevin was pointing at. "The rock cliff... right behind us."

"I know that," the boy said with disgust. "I mean this dark spot on the cliff."

Grant looked a little closer. "Probably just a shadow," he said as if to dismiss the inquiry.

Keith and Robby huddled around the open map to take a closer look.

"I never noticed that before," Keith said.

It did appear to be shadows cast by the uneven rock outcropping above it, but it also seemed more than just shadow, yet indistinct in nature. Robby studied the mysterious spot a few moments, and then walked over to the edge of the cliff. At his feet was a deep cavern carved into the hillside. A hundred feet or more below lay shale and boulders splayed out like a giant fan, mostly hidden by large timber. The face of the rock wall beneath him was not entirely visible, as it seemed to recess part-way down.

He returned to his seat, leaned against a tree, his mind grinding away at something profound. Keith and Grant patiently awaited the forthcoming revelation.

"A mineshaft," Robby mumbled. "It could be a mineshaft." He pondered some more as Grant and Keith went to peer over the edge of the cliff. They couldn't see the features of the wall below them, either, but they knew it was vertical.

"How could it be a mineshaft?" Grant asked. "No one could ever get to it."

"Cory Brockway told in his journal... the brief history of Silver Spring... remember?"

"Sort of..." Keith said.

Robby continued. "He said there was a mineshaft tunneled under the city... abandoned when it didn't produce anymore."

"I remember that," Grant said. "But Cory said that mine opening was on a steep hillside... not a cliff wall."

"D'ya see how the rocks at the bottom look like the leftovers of a landslide?" Robby asked them.

Grant and Keith looked again. "Yeah."

"That landslide has occurred *since* Clancy wrote this journal. He never once mentions anything about a sheer cliff next to the town... only steep hills."

"Guess that's possible," Keith said.

"What are you suggesting?" asked Grant.

"Let's look *outside* the box for a moment. If Clancy wasn't good at judging time, then Oliver might have had time to hustle the silver bars into an abandoned mineshaft. At that time, *before* the landslide, the mineshaft opening might have been easier to get to, but nobody would ever go there."

"We hafta take a look," Keith said.

Robby sprang to his feet and chased after Keith and Grant who were already on their way to get a better vantage point for viewing the rock wall.

"Why haven't we ever noticed this before?" Keith asked.

"For the same reason we can't see it now... trees!"

Trees *had* camouflaged the features of the landscape, just as the willows had hidden the little stream Robby discovered trickling out of the hillside behind Tanglewood. Just the top of the wall was visible from farther down the hill, and even at the bottom where they had camped—not enough to reveal the presence of a vertical cliff. Nowhere could they get a good look at it; either trees or the landscape kept it out of plain view. At the edge of the landslide about two-thirds of the distance down the hill, they finally got a peek. It seemed possible to climb a little closer from there, over the debris of the landslide, but it also appeared quite treacherous, and the contour of the cliff offered no guarantee that the shaft opening was actually there.

"I'll try it," Keith boldly declared. "I'll see if I can get up a little closer." He pulled the wrinkled T-shirt from the waistband of his jeans and slipped it over his head. Strong and agile, he was the best of the group to make the climb. He'd never tried rock climbing, though; this would be his first attempt.

Keith jumped down the six-foot drop at the edge of the landslide and started making his way toward the cliff. Large boulders and loose shale provided quite a challenge. Sound footing and handholds were scarce, and the shale pebbles were like trying to walk on marbles spread over a hockey rink.

"Can you see anything?" Grant called to Keith when it appeared that he might be at a better vantage point.

"NO!" was the only report.

Keith slowly kept progressing laterally, jumping from one boulder to the next. He was nearly to where he could see around the contour where the questionable dark spot was hiding. Another few feet and it would be visible to him. But he was running out of available solid surfaces on which to climb.

"I can just barely see it," he called back to the others. His voice echoed.

"What is it?" Grant shouted. "Does it look like a cave?"

"Can't tell for sure..." Keith stepped onto a bed of shale that extended fifty or sixty feet in a steep decline below him. In less time than it takes to slap a mosquito, Keith was sliding, tumbling, trying desperately to regain some control of his rapid descent.

"PUUUUUNKYYYYYY!" Kevin yelled, almost in tears. He envisioned Keith lying dead at the bottom of that ravine.

Grant and Robby didn't view it quite that seriously. "He's alright," Robby tried to comfort the boy.

When Keith got to his feet at the bottom, laughed, and shouted, "I'M OKAY... REALLY!" the rest of the boys laughed, too, relieved that injuries had not stopped the invincible Keith Bradley.

They reunited in the trees at the foot of the hill. Keith's clothes were a mess and he walked with a slight limp.

"Are you hurt? You're limping."

Keith winced. "I have a stone in my shoe."

THIRTY-EIGHT

Now it was time for a dip in the swimming hole before heading home. Keith was dirt from forehead to ankles, and the others were hot and sweaty, too. This was the day's highlight for Kevin.

After a good, long soak and a few laps around the hole, Keith and Robby climbed onto the bank while Grant and Kevin continued to play a game of submarine tag.

"So, what did you see on the cliff?" Robby asked as they perched on the bank with their bare feet dangling in the water.

"Couldn't really get a good look at it," Keith replied. "But it did seem like there might be a hole in the wall."

"How are we gonna find out?"

Keith furrowed his brow, deep in thought. "We could fly the chopper to it... shoot some pictures."

"That's a great idea!" Robby said.

"HEY! GRANT!" Keith called out.

Out in the middle of the pool, Grant broke his concentration on keeping track of his devious little brother, turned his attention toward the guys on the bank, and was immediately attacked from behind and drug down for a good dunking. But he came up laughing and then swam to the shore.

Robby thought it was a shame to interrupt their fun; he hadn't seen Grant enjoying Kevin's companionship this well in a long time.

"S'pose we could use the chopper and the remote camera one more time?"

"Sure. What d'ya wanna do?"

"Fly it up to the cliff wall and shoot some pics of our *black hole.*"

"Now that's a brilliant idea," Grant said. "We can do it right after the Fourth."

Oh, yeah. The Fourth. The grand barbeque. Any other time they would have had nothing else on their minds. For as long as they could remember, the Fourth of July barbeque was a major event of the year, ranking right up there with Christmas. It had started with just the three families together in one of their back yards, but then it began to grow with more invitations, and now, for the last two or three years it had expanded into all three back yards. The day-long party required a certain amount of preparation, much of which was the boys' responsibility. Lawns and gardens had to look their best; extra tables and chairs hauled in by a rental agency had to be positioned; badminton net in the Kraemer's yard, and volleyball court at the Bradley's.

The boys would see some of their friends from school among the many people who would come and go throughout the day; it would be a lot of fun and a lot of good food. And when it was all over, when twilight settled upon the town and serenity returned—the sky over the river would explode with FIREWORKS!

But right now, top priority was the trip home and Mrs. K's meatloaf. In the front seats Grant and Keith discussed getting the chopper ready and repositioning the camera to shoot straight forward instead of straight down; in the rear seats Robby and Kevin looked over the pocketful of coins Kevin had discovered.

Their first stop was at the Bradley house so Keith could get some clean clothes. Being Friday before a holiday weekend, Bill was home early; he sat at the kitchen table drinking coffee when the boys kicked their shoes off and Karen met them at the patio door.

"Good heavens! Punky," she exclaimed when she stared at the sorry state of Keith's clothes. "What happened to you?" She hadn't seen him this dirty since the boys were little, creating mud sculptures in the garden after a rain shower.

"Don't worry, Mom," Keith replied. "I'm clean underneath... we went swimming afterwards."

"Afterwards? After what?"

"After I slipped and slid down a sixty-foot long gravel hill."

"What were you doing on top of a gravel hill?"

"Looking for a hole in a rock cliff."

"A hole in a..." Mrs. B paused, thought the better of asking any more questions, and said: "Well, get those filthy clothes off and put them in the hamper down in the laundry room... *before* you set foot anywhere else in this house."

Bill Bradley sipped his coffee and laughed. "The most memorable days usually end with the dirtiest clothes," he said, more to Keith than to anyone else. He didn't know which was more amusing—Keith's forlorn appearance and his attempt at explaining, or his wife's hysterical antics and her attempt to understand.

"We're eating at my house," Grant volunteered as Keith trotted off to the basement laundry room.

"Mrs. K is making *meatloaf*," Robby added.

"Well, that works out just fine," Karen said. "Bill and I were thinking of going out for supper."

At the Gladstone house, they discovered that *all* the dads were home early for the holiday weekend. John and Earl were discussing some arrangements for the Sunday soirée and Phyllis was cleaning the kitchen counter after making one of her famous fruit salads.

"And where have you been all day?" she asked light-heartedly.

"Um... exploring," Robby said.

"Hmmm... you boys have been doing an awful lot of that lately... there can't be too much more uncharted territory left, is there?"

Robby laughed, and to avoid any more questions, he said: "We're eating supper at Grant's... Mrs. K is making meatloaf. I'm just gonna quick change my clothes." He hustled off to his room.

Keith sidled over to Phyllis and subtly tried to sneak a sample taste of the fruit salad. Before he could dip the spoon into the salad, she pushed the big bowl out of his reach. "Nice try, Prince Charming," Phyllis said with a grin. "That's for Sunday... you'll just have to wait."

"Aw, just one little taste?" Keith begged like a little kid. He loved her fruit salad.

"Oh, okay, Punky," Phyllis gave in to his magical boyish charm, faking pity and remorse. "Just one little taste... and then go away."

"Grant," Earl hailed his son. "They're bringing the tables over about three tomorrow afternoon. Can you be here to help put them in the yard? I'll be at Kevin's soccer game."

"Sure, Dad. Is everything else all set?"

"Think so... John and I hired a fry cook from the Country Chef to take care of the grills so we don't have to spend all day cooking this year."

"The Country Chef?" Grant gasped. "You mean fat, ugly, *grouchy* Bert is gonna cook our burgers?"

"No... not Bert... the young guy, Jeff. He's the only one who didn't have plans for the day."

Grant sighed relief. Bert wasn't too popular among the younger Wellington crowd. He growled at high schoolers when they came in for burgers and fries. But Jeff would be acceptable.

"Tell your mother when you get over there that I'll be home in a little while... after John and I finish our drinks."

John and Earl seemed to be in good spirits. Grant guessed it was probably their *second* Old Fashioned.

THIRTY-NINE

"The meatloaf was fan-tabulous as usual, Mrs. K," Keith complimented.

"Yes, Mrs. K, it was scrumptious," Robby added.

Kevin had already run off to get his soccer uniform ready for the next day when the other boys asked if they could help with the kitchen clean-up.

"Oh, no," Judy said. "I'll just put the dishes in the dish-washer. There's not much else to do. Did you get enough to eat?"

"Yes, Mom... thank you," the three boy choir sang out. Their bellies were full and satisfied, and now they thought they would settle into the den for a *Star Trek* episode on cable.

Earl joined them as he sometimes did. To make room for him Robby respectfully moved from the big comfy recliner to the couch with Grant and Keith.

"Haley Moore dropped by today," Earl said as he   lowered himself into the chair.

"*Sheriff* Haley Moore?" Grant questioned.   "What did he want?"

"I think he thought I should discipline you for going out to that place in the wilderness."

"Discipline us? Why? How did he know—"

"Seems your brother bragged to some of his buddies about the coins he found out there. Word got to the Sheriff somehow, and he doesn't think you should be going out there."

"Because of Mack," Robby mumbled. "Oh, God." He rolled his eyes and plopped against the sofa backrest.

"So we're not allowed to go out there anymore?" Keith asked.

"I didn't say that," Earl replied.

"But I thought you said the Sheriff told you—"

"Haley didn't say you *couldn't* go out there.   He said you *shouldn't* go out there... because it's dangerous."

"But it's not," Grant said.   "It's not much different than going to the park."

"I can believe that," Earl said.   "And I'm confident that you guys have enough common sense not to do something stupid... as long as you keep an eye on Kevin when he's with you... he hasn't quite matured yet, you know." He made eye contact with each of them to be sure they were paying attention.   "Haley realizes that there's no law keeping you out. It's public land and anyone can go there."

"Do you know about the legend?" Robby asked Earl.

"Yes, Robby, I've read all about it, and I don't know that I believe any of it. Seems like a bunch of hogwash to me."

"Some of it is," Robby said.   "We've already proved that Mack doesn't exist... never did." He decided at the last moment not to mention the mysterious music they had heard at the old hotel.

Earl leaned forward in his chair.   "Kevin told me just before supper that he found some more coins out there today."

"Yes, he did. A whole handful."

"He also told me that you guys have a map... that you're looking for some kind of *treasure* out there."

"It's *our* map," Grant said.   "The one we made with the photos from the helicopter... remember?"

"Yes, I do remember, and you figured out where everything was from some old diary. At least, that's what Kev told me."

"He told you right," Robby admitted.

"What's the treasure you think is out there?"

"Um... we're not absolutely sure... just kind of speculating... hunting. We're kinda keeping it our secret. Maybe Kev's already found our treasure."

"If he did," Earl mused, "I'll make him share it with you."

"Dad! Dad!" Kevin came busting in.   "Can we look up these coins on the internet?" He held out a cupped palm holding the heap of nickels and dimes.

"Do we have to do it tonight? I have my computer shut down."

"Pleeeeeeeeazzzz?"

Earl rose from the recliner. "Okay, let's go," he said to Kevin; he turned to the boys and winked. "Good luck with your hunt."

A while after Earl and Kevin had left, Robby contemplated the consequences of Kevin's knowledge of their secret mission. He didn't worry about Mr. K's awareness; he trusted their secret was safe with him. But if Kevin boasted in public about his additional finds, and happened to say something about treasure maps...

Robby verbalized his thoughts to Grant and Keith. "We need to keep him quiet."

Grant jumped up from the couch. "KEVIN!"

FORTY

Keith, Grant, and Robby put their usual effort into making the Fourth of July barbeque a success. Their   fathers looked on the event as a social offering to all of Wellington. They had created an Independence Day tradition; it seemed important to them. Dedication to the proper preparations usually was high priority, but this year, Kevin's soccer game held precedence over setting up extra picnic tables. There were three strong, responsible sons to take over.

Only because Kevin's soccer team, the Warriors, were considered the underdogs to the Red Hawk Wildcats, Bill Bradley and John Gladstone decided to devote a couple of hours to accompany Earl Kraemer on Saturday afternoon to watch the game and give a little added support. Soccer in Wellington wasn't yet considered a major sport, so unlike the Friday night football games in the fall when nearly every living creature in town turned out to cheer the home team, the boys on the soccer team appreciated even a small audience. Kevin, one of the designated strikers on the team, loved it when his dad was in the fan bleachers, and he would love it even more if he could kick in a scoring goal.

The four extra picnic tables arrived about 3:15, and by then, Robby and Keith had hauled ten cases of various flavored soda, thirty pounds of hamburger, six bottles each of mustard and catsup, and a gallon jar of dill pickles from the *Hy-Vee*. The moms had been busy all day producing enormous quantities of potato salad. The boys thought there was enough fare to feed half the city's population, and they sincerely hoped the *other* half didn't show up expecting dinner.

By that time, tour de force Kevin had scored two goals and the Warriors' 3-2 victory before a moderately larger-than-usual enthusiastic crowd sent the Wildcats back to Red Hawk with their tails between their legs and licking their wounds.

The larger crowd could be attributed to an earlier parade, softball games, small carnival, flea market and perfect weather that had drawn not only the Wellington residents, but visitors from a much larger area. City officials had made a good decision announcing the holiday activities to be held the day *before* the Fourth; Wellington wasn't competing with every other community in the entire country for its share of festival-goers. The only events reserved for Sunday were the continued carnival, two more softball games, and the Grand Finale of the weekend—the river fireworks display after sundown.

Grant, Keith, and Robby had their hands full containing Kevin when he and his jubilation exploded out of the car in the Kraemers' driveway. The dads enjoyed a sporting high, too, however, they refrained from performing outrageous war dances and yelping savage war whoops. Anyone in the entire neighborhood would find it difficult to nap right then with Kevin's high-octane celebration. Any other time, the dads might have put a stop to it, but this was a landmark accomplishment; never, in the relatively short soccer history in Wellington had they beaten the Wildcats!

Keith faked a comical British accent. "Must've been a bloody good footy match."

"It was quite a game," John said. "Kev kicked in a goal to tie the score just minutes after the second half kick-off, and then with less than a minute left in the game he intercepted a cross pass and slammed the tie-breaker... a thirty-yarder... caught their goalie completely off-guard. Yes! It *was a bloody good footy match!*"

Grant and Keith knew the joy of being the hero in a victory—catching a pass in the end zone for the winning touchdown, or sinking the tie-breaking three-pointer at the buzzer—and they knew how gratifying the attention from others felt afterward. They joined Kevin in the war dance, and Robby joined in, too, because he was happy for Kevin and because he was a part of the fraternity.

All the moms bounded from patio doors, abandoning their kitchens and potato salads, curious of the back yard commotion. It didn't take them long to figure out the state of affairs.

"Why didn't we just *buy* thirty pounds of potato salad and go to the game instead?" Phyllis cried.

FORTY-ONE

By four o'clock Sunday afternoon, the picnic crowd had thinned to just a few kids playing volleyball. The food, gone, the soda coolers, nearly empty, and four trash cans overflowing with paper plates, napkins and empty soda cans, John, Bill, and Earl sat at the patio table on the Gladstone deck, sipping their Scotch and water, something they had looked forward to for the last hour and a half. They complained about how much money the party had cost them, and then they laughed about it, anticipating a repeat next year. It had been a successful social event, and although it was not their primary reason for throwing such a party, the gratitude felt by neighbors and friends probably meant an increase in Sunflower Bakery bread sales, and a few additional investments to boost John's commissions. Earl, however, had little to gain; he didn't think there were too many people in Wellington who were building space shuttles or designing complicated communication centers. But he didn't care. Everyone had left happy, each one an intricate part of a more unified, friendly community, and to all three men on the patio, that mattered the most.

The boys sat on the riverbank long before dusk began covering everything with its invisible gray night shade. Vacant lawn chairs and spread blankets and quilts marked the spots so many people had secured earlier in the day to assure a perfect, unobstructed view of the patriotic light show.

"That's so stupid," Keith mumbled. "They could see fireworks from across town."

"Then... why are *we* here?" Grant asked.

"Well... at least we didn't bring lawn chairs and blankets down here twelve hours ago... and we still got a good spot to sit."

Kevin had joined up with his soccer buddies among the slowly gathering crowd; they were basking in the glory of stardom, with Kevin in the center spotlight—the first Wellington team ever to defeat the vicious Red Hawk Wildcats!

Robby suspected that the moms and dads were comfortably sprawled in chase lounges in the back yard with icy cocktails in hand, gazes nonchalantly fixed on the horizon toward the river. They would see the same fireworks from there, only with delayed sound effects. Somehow, though, this spot on the riverbank seemed better.

"Hey! I hear you're taking up ghost busting," a voice cut through the evening stillness. The boys turned to look for the source. It was Chad Bennett, one of their ex-classmates, known far and wide as a wise guy. "Did ya meet up with Mack yet?"

"Yeah," Keith responded instantly. "He wanted to know when we were bringing you out... he hasn't had a *Bennett* for dinner in quite some time."

Chad, apparently lacking a witty comeback, turned back to the group he was walking with and they all moved on.

"Good one," Grant congratulated Keith, and patted him on the back. They all had a good laugh.

"So, when should we go back out to Silver Spring?" Robby asked.

"When do you want to go? We should plan on camping next time."

"Is the helicopter ready to fly?"

"Just gotta charge the batteries. The camera mount is easy. I'll take my laptop along so we can see the pictures on a bigger screen without coming back home."

"We'll hafta help clean up the lawns," Keith reminded them.

"Yeah, but we can get all that done tomorrow."

"How 'bout leaving Wednesday or Thursday? We can stay the

whole weekend."

"Kevin won't be able to go with us," Grant said. "He has another *footy match* on Saturday... the Bedford Hurricanes."

Just then the distinct *"Rumpf!"* sounded from the explosive launch of the first skyrocket. They listened to the sizzle of the propellant and watched the barely visible trail of grayish smoke climb rapidly into the deep purple night sky. When it became silent, and they thought for sure it was a dud, a deafening boom shook the landscape and sent a tingling chill down every spine within earshot, signaling the beginning of a spectacular and noisy aerial show.

FORTY-TWO

A larger than usual crowd attending the Fourth of July barbeque meant a little more clean-up afterwards. Not as bad as the littered grounds left behind in the wake of a county fair, but a little trash here and there required raking that partially restored the grass where it was trampled down, too. In a few days, it would recover naturally on its own. The gas grills needed scrubbing and the badminton and volley ball nets were dismantled and returned to their storage spots in the garages until next year. The garbage collectors wouldn't have to guess why there were four large, extra trash cans at the curb—Roy and Herbert had been there on Sunday.

By Wednesday the whole town seemed to be back to its normal routines; youngsters cruised the streets on bicycles, scooters and skateboards; the working class had returned to their jobs; and retired folks relaxed in their porch swings and wicker rockers. The shopping center stores were running sales on all things red, white and blue—everything from bed linens and fly swatters to paper plates and parasols. Wellington had, once again, recovered from the influx of a temporarily larger population during the busy weekend.

Without drawing any abnormal attention, the boys casually announced that they would be going camping for a couple of nights.

"Where are you going this time?" Phyllis asked.

"Um... out to find more uncharted territory," Robby replied.

Earl just smiled when he saw the boys loading their camping gear and the helicopter into Grant's Jeep Wednesday evening. He knew Kevin wouldn't be joining them on this trip, as he had soccer practice on Thursday and another big match on Saturday. But Earl knew where they were going without asking. He was amused with their enthusiasm, impressed with their ingenuity, and fearful for their disappointment when their efforts produced nothing of value—a mythical treasure that he was certain didn't exist. But the boys were having a good time, and that's what he and the other dads and moms wanted them to do during this last summer together as kids. It was their reward for twelve years of extraordinary scholastic effort and achievements.

"We plan to be home for Kevin's soccer match on Saturday," Grant informed his dad. Never before had he or the other guys taken much interest in *"footy"* as they called it, but now, Kevin displayed promise as an athlete, even if it wasn't *their game*, and they were beginning to see the importance of their support.

Robby, Keith, and Grant had not given any thought to the impact that finding such an astronomical treasure would bestow on their lives. They had no idea of the legal hassle and the miles of red tape they would encounter. Perhaps they were subconsciously shielding themselves from the disappointments of failure that, in the back of their minds, they all knew to be a possibility. But for now, the adventure of the hunt, the adrenaline rush, the exhilaration was propelling them forward, for whatever results may come.

"Where are you gonna control the chopper from?" asked Robby as they peered at the hill from their campsite.

"I think from the top of the cliff," Keith replied. "It's the only place I'll be able to keep it in sight... don't want to crash it into the wall 'cause I can't see it. And Grant will have to be right there with me to shoot the pics."

It was just before noon when Keith launched the whirlybird into the air. This maneuver would require some precise flying, hovering the craft between the cliff and the treetops with the camera pointed in the proper direction. He had seen the face of the cliff a few days ago from below, and he knew the approximate location of the spot they wanted to photograph in relation to their position at the top of the cliff. He eased the chopper down into the cavern about fifty feet out from the face of the cliff where he could keep it easily within sight.

While it hovered in several different positions side to side and up and down, Grant clicked the photos; Robby watched with nervous anticipation, standing by with the laptop computer.

As soon as Keith set the helicopter down in a spot where they had cleared away the tall grass and weeds, Grant retrieved the memory card from the camera and plugged it into the slot on the laptop. Within a few seconds, they were staring at the pictures on the bigger screen.

"Looks like just shadows," Robby said, a little disappointed.

Grant gazed up into the sky. "If we wait 'til later when the sun gets more to the southwest… or maybe I could trigger the flash to eliminate the shadows."

Keith studied the darkest area on the screen. The photo that best showed the right portion of the rock wall was, at best, blurred, but there seemed to be more depth to that part of the shadow. He checked the clock that monitored flying time and battery life. "Nine and a half minutes," he said. "We've safely got seventeen or eighteen minutes left on this battery to try it again."

"Now?" Grant asked.

"Yeah… try your idea with the flash. If it doesn't work, we can try again later when the sun is right."

At this point, anything was worth a try. They had nothing to lose. Grant reinstalled the memory card in the camera. When he was back at the edge of the cliff ready for action, Keith returned the chopper back to its hovering status with the camera lens facing the cliff wall. Again, Grant shot another series of pictures, and this time, because he was using the flash, he stepped up the camera shutter speed, attempting to achieve sharper clarity in the images.

The adrenaline was pumping as they huddled at the computer, staring, waiting for each picture to load onto the screen. When the right photo came up, hands slapped together in high-fives and the boys rejoiced in their greatest discovery so far. Clearly, without a doubt, the dark spot—their *black hole* that was visible only on a picture—was truly a passageway into the bowels of the earth. Had they discovered the lost mine shaft?

FORTY-THREE

There was no doubt in their minds that they had discovered the best hiding spot—Oliver's vault—for the stolen silver ingots. What the picture revealed *had* to be the abandoned mine shaft. It had been a good choice for Oliver; he knew no one had any interest in going there for any reason. Even Clancy had determined that. And in later years, Mother Nature had insured the safety of whatever might be hidden there by cutting off the only access with a landslide. That's why Cory Brockway had not found it. That's why *no one* had ever stumbled onto it. It was just too well concealed.

That is... until three curious, industrious boys plus one inquisitive little brother came along with the ability to eke out the clues. But now that they had found the most probable cache, getting to it and investigating its contents would prove to be a gargantuan challenge.

The boys cooled off in the swimming hole. The mine shaft was totally inaccessible to them; there was nothing more to do, now, without further planning.

"How are we gonna get in there to check it out?" Robby asked as they relaxed in the coolness of Silver Creek.

That was a question that had presented itself to all three.

They recognized the element of danger in attempting to reach the mine shaft opening. Keith had already proven that; climbing up to it from the bottom appeared next to impossible. By the pictures that revealed the features of the cliff face, there didn't seem to be any ledges that would accommodate an approach from either side.

"The only way possible," Keith suggested, "is to repel down to it from the top."

"You mean with ropes?"

"Yeah."

"Looks and sounds dangerous."

"Got any better ideas?"

Grant had been pondering on the possibilities, too. "I think we should study the pictures some more. I can enhance the photos on the computer at home... so we can get a better image of what we're dealing with."

"Think we should try to get some more pictures?" Keith asked.

"Won't hurt to get some from different angles," Grant replied. "But let's do it tomorrow afternoon when the sun is on the cliff. Too late today... it's in shadow, now, from the trees."

FORTY-FOUR

Kevin was ecstatic to see Grant at home on Friday evening. "Coming to the game tomorrow?" he excitedly asked his big brother.

"Yeah... sure."

"How 'bout Robby and Punky?"

"You should stop calling him *Punky*."

"Why?"

"'Cause he doesn't like it. Only the moms are allowed to call him that."

"But Robby does."

"Only when he's talking to you. He *never* says it around Keith."

"Okay... are Robby and *Keith* coming?"

"Yes... we're all going to your footy match."

"Were you out at the haunted place again?"

Grant nodded.

"Did ya find the treasure yet?"

"No."

"Gonna look some more?"

"Yeah."

"When?"

"Don't know... we hafta study the new pictures we took

today."

"Pictures of what?"

"The rock cliff."

"Oh... that dark spot I saw on the map?"

"Yeah."

"Did ya use the helicopter again?"

"Yeah."

"Think that's where the treasure is?"

"Maybe."

"How are you gonna get to it?"

"That's why we have to study the pictures."

"Can I see them?"

"They're not downloaded from the camera yet."

"Well, when they are, can I see them?"

"Sure."

Kevin seemed to run out of questions. He scurried off to get his team uniform ready for the next day. Grant went to his room to work on the pictures until dinner was ready.

Robby had always been more tolerable of Grant's little brother, and he had always found value in their friendship. He had also attended more of Kevin's *footy* matches in the past. Grant had watched a few, and Keith had seen two or three. None of them had ever played, but they were sports-minded boys so they had a fair appreciation of the game.

By the fifteen-minute halftime break, the Warriors trailed the Bedford Hurricanes 1-0. The dads were feeling a little edgy because this opposing team had never been so challenging to the Warriors. But they remembered the strong come-back in the second half of the Wildcats game, and that seemed to restore their confidence.

Grant, Robby, and Keith needed to satisfy their thirst; they strolled over to the Boy Scouts' mobile concession stand, a small enclosed trailer with a large window and counter on one side. While standing in line waiting for sodas, Grant noticed a dark green Ford truck in the parking lot. He recognized it as belonging to someone in the four-wheel-drive club, but he couldn't put a face on the owner. He scanned the crowd, but no one jogged any familiar memories that he could associate with the group.

When they rejoined the dads on the bleachers, the kick-off had just gotten the second half under way. The Warriors had controlled the ball for a couple of minutes when 'Taz' Martin received a cross pass from Kevin and kicked it past the goalie into the net to tie the score. The hometown fans cheered as they watched Taz do his little ego dance on the field.

The rest of the game was a battle to the death with a team that had obviously improved since their last engagement with the Warriors. In the last minutes the Hurricanes appeared to be in control of the game. But then, like a secret weapon in reserve, once again, Tour de force Kevin rushed in to intercept a pass and sent a scorching twenty-yard kick between the uprights, far out of reach for the defending goalie. Seconds later the final whistle sounded. Kevin's was more than an ego dance—it was a victory dance.

The small crowd of spectators cheered as loudly as a small crowd can, and within a few minutes it had dispersed. The boys waited for Kevin to join them, but he was too engaged with his teammates celebrating the victory.

Grant looked to the parking lot, hoping to see the owner of the green Ford truck, but it was already gone.

FORTY-FIVE

"We can drop a rope down this side," Grant said, pointing to the computer screen. "There seems to be some footing right there, next to the opening."

Keith and Robby leaned in closer to examine the pictures. From two different angles, a ledge did appear to be present— narrow, but wide enough to provide a step.

"Of course," Grant continued. "There's no guarantee that it's solid... by the looks of it, this whole cliff is nothing but shale and sandstone; that's why part of it slid away. Burrowing the mine shaft probably weakened the hill and in time this outer surface just caved in."

"What if," Keith said and then he pondered a moment. "What if the part of the shaft where Oliver hid the bars went down with the landslide? That would mean our treasure is at the bottom of that hill... buried under—"

"I doubt it," Robby cut in. "If you look at the contour of the hill on either side of the landslide, there's not but fifteen or twenty feet of hill missing, and there would have been some sort of level entryway dug back into the hillside in front of the tunnel opening. Not much of the shaft is actually missing, and I don't think Oliver would've put it just inside the door... he would've taken it back farther... way out of sight."

"Well, we won't know until we take a look," Keith said.

"We need to get some equipment together," Grant suggested.

"Right. What do we need?"

"For starters... rope... lots of it."

"And we gotta remember to take some good flashlights," Robby added.

"We need something better than just flashlights," Keith said.

"A high-powered lantern is what we need."

"And leather gloves... and sweatshirts," Robby said. "It'll be cold in that mine shaft."

They discussed their supply needs and method of operation including climbing techniques well into the night. When Kevin begged to see the new pictures and he was admitted into the room, he stared at the monitor screen for a while without any comment.

"Wanna come with us to check out the old mine shaft?" Robby asked.

Kevin shook his head wildly. "No way! You guys are crazy! No way I'm gonna climb down that cliff."

"Suit yourself," Grant said. "But just remember what we told you about keeping your mouth shut about this."

"My lips are zipped." Kevin pressed his thumb and forefinger together and swiped them across his mouth, as if closing a zipper. He knew they were serious.

The other three went to their comfortable beds that night confident that their next trip to Silver Spring would be rewarding, or, at least, exciting.

FORTY-SIX

A **high powered lantern** and leather gloves purchase might not have seemed out of the ordinary, but one hund-red feet of heavy rope did raise some eyebrows at the hardware store. Uncertain whether or not Kevin's chatter about where they had been "exploring" had circulated throughout the town, the boys had to be cautious wher-ever they went. They had noticed a few sideways glances and even a couple of pitiful frowns, as if they were doomed to be Mack's next victims. Apparently, there were a few people in the town who were aware of their visits to a place that had remained taboo down through the ages. It was nearly impossible for anyone living here now to recall any firsthand knowledge of Silver Spring, and it seemed highly unlikely that many would even remember the incidents connected to it that occurred in 1968. Obviously, though, the legend had survived among the older generations and certain warnings had been passed on in some social circles. Some knew of its location, but it was a safe bet that no one living in Silver Spring at present had ever actually left a footprint on that hill—except Robby, Grant, Keith, and Kevin—and it was also a safe bet that no one was, or ever had been aware of the possible treasure that lay hidden there. If they had, some daring, foolish soul would have attempted to recover it, regardless of the *dangers* that might befall him while trespassing on Mack's territory. Yes, clearly there were those aware of the boys' escapades, and although the opinions were never voiced, noticeable disapproval seemed to latently exist.

But at Abbey's Café everything appeared quite normal. Ranch Burgers and Curly Fries seemed the best way to satisfy the appetites they had acquired during their Monday morning shopping spree.

"So are we gonna camp again? Or should we just go for the day?" was the general conversation once the burgers and fries were ordered. After a long discussion on the subject, it was decided to just plan a day trip, so they   weren't so crowded in the Jeep with all the camping gear. It would be just the three of them, as Kevin was too involved with becoming the next World Class Soccer star; individual practice with a couple of teammates throughout the week, formal team practice on Thursday, and another match on Saturday.

"Are we going to Kevin's game on Saturday?" Robby asked.

"It's at Elk Creek," Grant said.

"That's seventy miles from here!"

"Yeah... still wanna go?"

Robby's forehead wrinkled in a frown. "Saturday's a long ways off... let's wait and see."

More properly outfitted for some serious climbing—hiking boots instead of sneakers and jeans instead of shorts—on Wednesday they chose a different path up the hill to reach the plateau; still a steep climb, it was closer to the edge of the recently discovered landslide and the cliff. Lodgepole pines towered above them and the tilted landscape was littered with jagged, irregular boulders and rocks of various sizes. Sun shafts filtered down through the forest canopy feeding the lush green grass and abundant yellow wildflowers. Dark-crowned Chickadees flittered about overhead, chattering gaily as if thrilled to have visitors. Ground squirrels scampered from rock to rock, ahead of the invaders, but bold enough to stick around. Even though there had not been measurable rainfall in quite some time, the place smelled fresh and clean.

Half-way up the hill Robby stopped to take in the beauty and the calming serenity. Grant and Keith halted the climb, as well. They all sat down on boulders for a little break, entertained by the noisy scolding from the gophers sitting on their haunches atop nearby rocks, some of the less brave stretching like furry little periscopes out of the long grass, curiously watching the aliens.

"Have you ever noticed?" Keith said as they rested. "That there's hardly ever any flies or bugs around here?"

"It's probably the loosestrife," Robby informed him.

"Huh?"

"Loosestrife... the yellow wildflowers that are so plentiful here. Look around... they're all over."

Keith and Grant scanned the area, taking notice of the bright yellow blossoms that were indeed quite numerous.

"So... what do the yellow flowers have to do with it?" Grant asked.

"Loosestrife," Robby explained, "Was tied in bunches and hung around draft horses' necks during the hot summer months to keep the flies and other insects from irritating them... and the fragrance even soothed and calmed the animals, too."

It didn't surprise the other two that Robby could recite such trivial information; he was, by far, the star history and science scholar among them, but Keith was curious how he had attained this astounding bit of data.

"I looked it up after we were here the first time," Robby replied to the inquiry. "I was curious about all the yellow flowers... didn't know what they were, so I looked it up."

They all sat there for a little while, enjoying this bucolic, bug-free utopia, wishing they could just stay there for eternity.

"It's a shame, ain't it?" Robby said. "That this place is going to waste."

"No," Grant responded. "Better for us... just think what thousands of people tramping through here would do to it." He gazed out over the valley, Silver Creek threading its private, sparkling journey among the hills, lingering every so often to form a secluded pool in which to entertain its grateful but infrequent guests with a cooling, soothing retreat from the hot afternoon sun.

"I guess you're right. If only people could enjoy something

like this without destroying it."

"Nobody else *could* enjoy it," Keith said. "They'd be too busy being afraid of their own silly legend."

"All the better for us," Grant said again.

"Well, shall we continue our mission?" Robby suggested. "Before the hoards start showing up?"

Keith replaced the heavy coil of rope over his shoulder. Grant and Robby picked up the lantern, water jug, and backpack containing additional flashlights, leather gloves, three hoodie sweatshirts, their map and the cliff pictures. They resumed the trek up to the top.

FORTY-SEVEN

"Gentlemen?" Grant announced as he stood gazing over the rim of the cliff that now was beginning to look like the summit of a Grand Canyon wall. Until now, the adventure had proven relatively tame in terms of physical danger, but now the reality of risking their safety loomed just inches away. "Before us lies our greatest challenge. And let's just hope that it becomes our greatest accomplishment."

Keith scanned the horizons; he was experiencing that uneasy sensation again, but not because of the potentially hazardous climb down the face of the cliff. He looked at Robby, and he could tell that Robby, too, was slightly on edge. But because they both knew that Grant would scoff at their paranoia, neither of them said anything.

One end of the rope was securely fastened to a substantial oak tree twenty feet back from the edge of the cliff. Referring to the pictures in order to accurately locate their target, the remaining coil was tossed over the cliff, immediately disappearing from sight. They had already agreed that Keith would make the first descent down the cliff; he was the strongest and most able for such a feat. He donned a pair of leather gloves, stuffed one of the small flashlights in his hip pocket, gripped the rope, and backed cautiously to the edge of the cliff. As he stepped over finding solid footing and leaning back with the rope supporting his weight, he began the backward walk down the sheer rock wall. There were no well wishes of good luck from the other two: they didn't believe in luck. Their disciplined sports training had taught them that luck was something you either earned or invented through strength of character; you developed the results of your efforts with courage and skill; you had to come by it honestly; you didn't trick or bluff your way into it. All three were strong advocates of that concept.

Carefully guiding himself downward, Keith soon disappeared from Grant's and Robby's sight. Each step backward was placed with prudence as he calculated each downward move. He'd been at the bottom of that cliff, and he had no desire to be there again. From this height, even landing in the nearly vertical bed of shale

gravel wouldn't be pleasant. It wouldn't necessarily be a fatal fall, but it *certainly* wouldn't be pleasant.

Robby and Grant scarcely breathed while they waited and peered over the edge. There really was no point in watching as they knew Keith

would be entirely out of their line of sight for the duration of his probe. But they watched anyway out of anxious anticipation, waiting what seemed to be hours for a vocal report. In real time, however, it was only a matter of several minutes when they heard the first dispatch from Keith.

"OKAY," he shouted. "I'M AT THE SIDE OF THE MINE SHAFT." There was a long pause. "LOOKS LIKE WE WERE WRONG ABOUT THAT LEDGE." Another long pause. "I'M GONNA JUST SWING MYSELF OVER TO THE OPENING."

Robby and Grant could hear what sounded like the scuffing of shoes and small rocks bouncing down the face of the lower cliff, and then the rope seemed to go slack for a moment, only to tighten again, but there was no vocal report from Keith right away.

"YOU OKAY?" Robby yelled, but his request yielded no response.

"KEITH! ARE YOU OKAY?"

Keith had landed himself on the entrance floor of the mine shaft with little difficulty and secured the rope end by weighting it with a rock. In awe of the sight before him, he took a few steps in, completely oblivious to the frantic shouts from above. He pulled the flashlight from his back pocket and pointed it forward into the tunnel. The light beam reflected off something shiny, bouncing back into the hazy blackness beyond. Keith's heart did a back flip in his chest and he couldn't breathe. A few more steps toward the puzzling shimmer, however, brought him back to breathing normally again. It was only a pool of water.

The small flashlight's beam wasn't strong enough to entirely illuminate the interior of the shaft, but it appeared to continue on for quite some distance, the walls and ceiling supported by large wooden beams. He could hear water trickling, and that accounted for the pool in front of him, but he couldn't determine where it was coming from, or where it was going away from the pool. It had to be draining somewhere.

Then he heard the faint shouts from Grant and Robby. He had penetrated the tunnel far enough that their voices were muffled and he realized that he had not reported to them after he was safely inside the mine shaft. He hustled back to the opening where the temperature rose many degrees and the bright sunlight nearly blinded him.

"KEITH! ARE YOU OKAY?" came another hysterical call from Grant.

"YEAH... I'M FINE! JUST DANDY!"

"YOU HAD US WORRIED."

"SORRY... I WENT BACK INTO THE TUNNEL A WAYS... DIDN'T HEAR YOU."

"SO WHAT DO YOU SEE DOWN THERE?"

"I'M COMING BACK UP... I'LL TELL YOU THEN."

Keith grabbed the rope tightly and swung himself over to the side of the opening where he started his 'walk' up the face of the cliff, pulling himself hand-over-hand with the rope. At the top, Grant and Robby were right there to assist him over the edge.

"It's quite easy to get into," Keith reported. "Just let yourself down easy, step carefully, and when you see you're beside the opening just push yourself away from the wall with your feet and swing over to the shaft." And then as an afterthought he warned: "But last man down... don't let go of the rope once you're in. It'll swing back over... out of reach... so hang onto it... weight it down with a rock."

"Okay, so what did you see in there?"

"Couldn't see much with the little flashlight, but it looks like it goes back a long ways."

"Are we gonna hafta crawl?"

"No," Keith replied. "It's high enough to walk as far as I could see, but be prepared to get wet."

"Wet? Why?"

Keith was already on his way to the trees searching for a fallen branch that he could trim and use as a probe for depth of the water pool in the tunnel. He explained while he worked. "The pool looks like it's only about ten feet across in that one spot, and then the water seemed to be all to one side after that... as far as I could see."

"Ground water," Robby said. "When you dig that deep into the earth, you're bound to hit ground water somewhere."

"And Robby?" Keith said. "You were right about it being cold in there. Man! It's like a deep freeze!"

"That far underground," Robby said, "It should be a constant forty-five degrees... year 'round."

"Well, I'm just glad you convinced us to bring sweatshirts. We'll definitely need 'em."

Keith had his probing stick all prepared. He turned to the others. "Okay, guys. You ready to go find some treasure?"

FORTY-EIGHT

"The backpack is gonna be a little bulky to handle climbin' down that rope," Robby complained.

"Then leave it here," Grant suggested.

"No," Robby insisted. "This is all the stuff we decided that we need."

"I agree with Robby," Keith said. "We should take it with us." He wasn't necessarily concerned about the backpack. But he, like Robby, didn't want to leave anything behind because of the uneasy feelings of the presence of other beings in their midst.

Grant sensed that Robby might be a little unsure of himself navigating down the cliff on the rope. "Okay," he said. "I'll take the pack. We'll tie the lantern to your belt loop. It doesn't weigh much at all."

That seemed an agreeable trade to Robby. Grant tied the lantern to a belt loop in the back so it would be completely out of the way, causing no interference with Robby's maneuvering ability on the rope.

When they were all ready for the climb, Keith saw that Robby was a little nervous. "It's really easy," he said to Robby. "Easier than the rope climb in gym class. You remember that, don't you?"

Robby nodded.

"I'll go down first," Keith said. "I'll be right there to help you... if you need it... when you get to the opening."

Robby wasn't exactly scared, but he was a little embarrassed that he might be somewhat of a burden to the others. He knew his athletic ability wasn't as sharp as theirs.

"You okay with this?" Keith asked once more.

Robby nodded.

"You ready, then?"

Robby nodded again.

Keith grasped the rope and slowly eased himself over the edge, keeping an eye on Robby, as to give him some last minute demonstrative instructions. Then he was out of sight. Only a few minutes had passed when he called out: "OKAY, ROBBY... COME ON DOWN."

Robby was plagued with mixed emotions; he was eager to do this, but apprehension held him back for a moment. Then his gloved hands reached for the rope and he summoned up all his courage. Stepping back off the edge and leaning against the rope, just like he had watched Keith do twice, he began his downward ply. Sweat was rolling off every inch of his body by the time he reached the spot where he saw Keith waiting for him. His motions hadn't been as graceful as Keith's, he was sure, but he had made it this far.

"Okay," Keith said calmly. "Push yourself out and toward me... let yourself swing over here."

Robby hesitated a moment and then gave a push with his feet. His swinging arc fell a little short of his target; he planted his feet against the wall, and the angle of the rope pulled him back to his original position.

"Try it again," Keith said. "Push a little harder this time."

Robby followed the instructions and gave a mighty shove. He surprised himself with the ease of reaching the shelf where Keith stood. Keith grabbed one arm to steady him as he lit on the mine shaft floor.

A big smile came to Robby. "Whew... I don't know what I was so worried about," he sighed. "That was really easy."

"Told ya," Keith grinned. "OKAY, GRANT... COME ON DOWN."

Grant's descent was similar to Robby's in duration and degree of caution. But when he arrived alongside the shaft opening, he saw what he had to do. His long legs bent at the knees and like coming off a spring board he sent himself in a wide swinging arc, came into the mine shaft mouth like a fighter jet landing on an aircraft carrier, overshot and sprawled on the floor six feet beyond where Robby and Keith stood waiting to assist. Robby grabbed the rope before it swung back out of reach.

A few laughs were in order, but the laughs were more congratulatory gestures to each other; they had successfully achieved the first difficult goal, but they suspected it was not the last.

FORTY-NINE

Grant got to his feet and quickly removed the backpack, dropping it to the ground. "WOW!" he said when Keith trained the high-powered light beam into the tunnel. Keith had seen it before, and Robby had taken a sneak peak while they waited for Grant to descend the cliff. But this was Grant's first look.

The eight-foot-wide tunnel appeared to have at least a six-foot ceiling, more or less, well-supported by heavy wooden timber uprights on either wall and equally heavy beams spanning across. The stronger light revealed more clearly now that the passageway gradually made a turn to the left about two hundred feet in. At less than half that distance was the pool that Keith had described, and beyond that, a stream of water contained within a trench close to the left wall. A hazy fog hung above the pool at the point where the warm outside air entering from the tunnel mouth collided with the cool underground atmosphere, condensing the dense moisture to visible fog. The dirty brown walls and ceiling reflected nothing, absorbing the light, offering nothing more than the appearance of a long-forgotten dungeon. Hash marks made by now-faded chalk, hundreds of them, in the traditional group of four with a strike-through to indicate five decorated the walls. An occasional set of initials and a scribed number—a date, perhaps—accompanied the tally marks here and there, but it would have been difficult to decipher their

172

meaning.

To anyone else, it might have appeared as a spooky, dismal, dreary cellar; to the boys, though, it was the setting for intrigue.

The need for the sweatshirts became strikingly evident as they neared the pool. The outside eighty degrees abruptly and drastically dropped, causing little hesitation to bring out the warmer attire. Now, with the sweats on, they thought they were prepared for the journey to the center of the earth.

Shoulder to shoulder they proceeded toward the pool, Keith advancing just a little with his long probing stick as they approached. He stabbed the stick into the water in random spots; the pool deepened to the left, but on the far right side the water was only three or four inches deep. Stepping as far to the right as possible, he started across, probing with the stick directly ahead, making certain of solid footing. In single file, Robby and Grant followed, thankful that they had thought to wear waterproof hiking boots instead of sneakers. The water was cold.

They had walked only ten yards beyond the pool when appeared on their right a wide arched opening. From that point forward, what they had thought to be the mineshaft wall was actually a row of upright timbers in perfect line, and from a distance had appeared as a wall. Behind them was a cavernous room at least sixty to eighty feet long and fifty feet wide, the ceiling vaulting ten or twelve feet above the floor.

"Why would there be this big room?" Keith asked no one in particular.

"They must've found an extremely rich silver vein in this direction," Robby explained. "They kept digging here until it ran out."

The dirt and rock floor was relatively flat and level, save for the far right side where it tapered down and eventually met with another large pool of black water. Robby and Grant each retrieved a small flashlight from the backpack, and they all toured the room, shining their lights over every inch of its interior. They realized, now, that their hunt for treasure had also become a learning experience, as well.

When they had satisfied their curiosity in the large cavity, finding nothing but a few chalk marks on the wall, and some abandoned broken tools, they continued on toward the bend in the tunnel. Peering back to the entrance, they were more than two hundred feet into the earth, and the angle of the shaft had taken them slightly upward.

The curve of the tunnel was less abrupt than they had anticipated, and just beyond where they lost sight of the thimble of entrance light, there opened up another large cavern to the left, similar to the first one they had thoroughly examined, but only half the size. In this one, the ceiling tapered down from twelve feet at the main passageway side to only three feet at the back.

"Must not've found as much here," Grant said as he paced along near the back wall where the ceiling still offered enough clearance for his height. Again, they inspected every nook and crevice, but with much less success than the miners had. A smashed oil lantern was the only point of interest.

Another hundred feet farther, the entire tunnel widened into a large cathedral-like room; the ceiling domed upward fifteen feet or more, the oval-shaped chamber at least eighty feet across at its widest point. Here the water flowed along two channels cut into the solid rock floor; one which the boys had been following ever since they had crossed the obstructing pool just inside the entrance; another flowed off to the right, its trench, too, cut into solid rock. Searching this huge area found only two corridors leading away from it: the left one being the source of the water flowage; the one to the right carrying the second water stream into more mysterious darkness.

Huddled together at the center with a stream on either side, they stared at the dirty, lifeless brown walls, a slight tinge of discouragement falling upon them.

"Do you feel that?" Keith said.

"What?" Grant replied quickly.

"Be real still. There's a slight... I can feel... I can feel air moving."

The others stood like courthouse statues, their flashlight beams streaking out like 1950s searchlights advertising a drive-in theater.

"There," Keith said again. "Do you feel it?"

"Yeah," Grant said.

Robby nodded in agreement. "For air to be moving in here, there must be another opening somewhere... which makes sense. There would have to be some sort of ventilation..."

"Or an escape route," Keith suggested. They had avoided speaking of the possibility of a cave-in, but it did exist.

"Where d'ya think it's coming from?"

"Don't know... hard to tell."

The large chamber where they stood was the junction of two passages. They stared at one, and then the other.

Keith pointed the high-powered light to the one on the left, the source of the water flow. "Let's try that one first," he said, and started walking toward it.

Within another hundred feet they had encountered four more widened areas and chambers, obviously where the silver vein had fanned out. All these areas were scrutinized, but nothing more than the usual broken and abandoned tools and an occasional smashed oil lamp. They noticed here, too, that the air seemed dead and stale, stagnant. But the water still flowed.

Not much farther into that corridor, the answer to the dead air question revealed itself. The boys stood and stared at the rubble—stones and boulders, shale and sand, broken and splintered timbers—the heap of which completely closed off the tunnel.

A few moments passed in silence. Robby finally spoke. "Clancy wrote about mineshaft cave-ins."

"Suppose this happened after Oliver hid the silver?"

"No," Robby replied. "This happened while the mine was still operating… probably why it was shut down."

"How do you know that?"

Robby pointed his light beam on the ground at the foot of the rubble pile. "See that?" he said. "Rails for the ore carts… like a small-scale railroad. They're missing in all the rest of the tunnel… been taken out after the mine was closed… except here."

Two stubs of steel track protruded from the rubble, at which point they had become impossible to recover. Near the top of the heap, three wooden crosses had been placed, now covered by a century of dust. It was quite clear that this had been the end of the line for at least three silver miners.

"Somewhere back in there are the bones of three men," Keith said somberly.

No one responded. They just turned and headed back to the junction.

FIFTY

They had been overcome with sadness at the thought of the men they didn't even know who were buried under that pile of stone and shale. The men had no names, and their lives had ended over a century in the past. There was no reason for the boys to feel so hurt by such an event that happened so long ago, but they still felt saddened. They had made a connection with Silver Spring and its people, and they felt like they *were* a part of it.

"Okay," Keith said when they reached the point where the streams split. "Let's forget about the bodies back there and follow this other stream." He pointed the light into that corridor and they cautiously pressed into the dark tunnel.

This passage offered less overhead clearance; Grant had to stoop most of the time, and in a few places even Robby and Keith, who were both nearly a head shorter than Grant, had to duck to avoid massive concussions.

Only one expanded area where the miners had dug off in tangents lay between the junction and what the boys suspected to be another collapsed shaft. But this blockage appeared singularly unlike the first.

There was no rubble here; the wall and ceiling beams were all intact, undisturbed. The very large stones blocking this passageway appeared as though they had been purposely put there, stacked in an orderly fashion, unlike the catastrophic ruins they had observed before.

Robby thought he saw something peculiar and he climbed up on the first layer of rocks for a closer look. He put his face up to the wall of rocks while Grant and Keith watched, thinking that he had suddenly lost control of his senses.

"What are you doing?" Grant asked.

Robby came away from the rocks smiling. "Does it seem a little warmer here?" he said.

"Now that you mention it, yeah."

"That's because on the other side of those rocks it's eighty degrees." Robby pointed and then explained that he had noticed a pinpoint of light between two of the big rocks. "When I looked, I could see out... and we're under the hillside behind Tanglewood. I recognize the little stream under the willow trees I found out there the day you were taking pictures with the chopper. This is the other entrance."

The boulders that Robby had seen that day containing a pool of spring water were also the boulders that blocked the mineshaft entrance, except he didn't realize it, or even suspect it that day. The large rocks weren't stacked so snugly as to be air-tight. Keith and Grant agreed that there was a measureable draft of warm air rushing in, but the underground coldness quickly reduced its temperature as it moved through the mine tunnel.

Grant and Keith both took turns at peering out through the tiny hole to confirm Robby's report.

"We'd need a pretty good pry bar to move these rocks," Keith commented.

"Why would we want to move them?" Robby asked.

"To open up the entrance."

"*Not* a good idea," Robby responded. "That entrance was blocked for a reason... and I think *we* have a good reason to leave it that way."

"Which is..."

Robby nearly whispered, as if someone might be eaves-dropping. "The treasure."

"But there's nothing here," Grant interjected. "We've covered this whole mineshaft and all the off-shoots. We haven't found anything but some broken old tools and a whole lot of dark. There's nothing here."

"Oh, but it's here," Robby disagreed. "The silver is here... I can feel it. We just haven't found it yet." Robby just then realized that *his* next difficult task was to convince Grant and Keith that they shouldn't give up just yet.

FIFTY-ONE

They made their way back through the mineshaft, continuously raking every surface with the lights, searching for a corner or a hole in the wall that they might have missed during the first pass.

"By the way," Keith said. "What are we looking for? I mean... how big *is* a seventy-pound bar of silver?"

"It's about the size of a fourteen-inch-long two-by-four," Robby explained. "And after all this time, they will probably appear black in color from a tarnish that has oxidized the outer surface."

By the time they waded across the pool and sat down near the mouth of the mineshaft, they felt somewhat exhausted. They had found nothing. Silence prevailed for a few minutes while they passed around the water jug. Sweatshirts peeled off in the warmer air to cool the topsides, and the boots came off to warm their cold, wet feet.

"I think I would've liked to live in Silver Spring," Keith said to break the quiet.

"Why do you say that?" Grant asked.

"I've been imagining the streets and all the old buildings... what it all looked like; and all the people that Clancy described, and the way of life he wrote about, and just think about what a neat place this is. Just seems like it would've been a great place to live."

"It's a neat place *now*, but a hundred years ago it might not've been the same."

"Fewer trees, maybe, but the hill was here and the creek ran in the valley just like it does now, and—"

Grant interrupted. "And dusty when it was dry and muddy when it rained, no electricity, no cars, and gunfights in the street," he pointed out.

"Yeah... wouldn't it be great?"

"Sounds like a rough life to me."

"Rough, maybe by our standards of today, but back then they prob'ly thought they had it pretty good. And remember," Keith added. "There was a lot of money in this town. The people who lived here prob'ly had as much luxury as anywhere else at that time."

Robby kept staring at the chalk marks on the wall. There was just enough light where the boys sat for the writing to be visible, but not bright enough to see the detail of the initials and numbers that Robby knew were there. He pointed his flashlight at the wall, but the batteries were weak by this time and the beam did little. So he reached for the high-powered lantern, switched it on, and flooded the wall with bright light.

All the markings seemed to be grouped in some sort of organized fashion. They were more than just a crude prison cell wall calendar that simply marked off the days. These markings had meaning—perhaps a means of temporarily recording units of production or something of that nature. Neither Cory Brockway nor Clancy Crane had written anything in their journals to indicate what such a record signified, and as Robby thought about it, he decided that it was nothing to be concerned about now. He switched off the light.

"So," Grant said. "D'ya think we should start looking some more up in the foundation rocks?"

Robby rubbed his chin and stared at his feet, unsure of his answer right away. "I don't know," he finally mumbled. "I don't think we're gonna find anything there. I still think it's in this mineshaft... makes more sense."

"But Robby... we've looked everywhere in here... twice..."

"We're just missing something—just like we missed something on the map before."

"Well, anyway... it must be getting late 'cause I'm getting hungry," Keith said. "What d'ya say we head home and come back to look some more another day?"

That was a most agreeable suggestion. Without any further discussion on the matter, they gathered up their gear and prepared for the rope climb back to the top of the cliff.

Grant was the first to swing out from the tunnel. Robby had less trouble this time, and for Keith, it was just another walk in the park.

FIFTY-TWO

The seventy-mile drive to Elk Creek on Saturday turned out to be rather enjoyable in the yellow Mustang convertible. The boys had made this trip many times, but it had always been on a team bus for football and basketball games. Kevin was on a bus that day, and because of his rapid rise into soccer stardom, the moms as well as the dads were eager to attend the game at Elk Creek, too; they were all travelling together in the Kraemers' nine-passenger conversion van. There would have been room for the boys, but they opted for their own ride, suggesting that it would be more comfortable for the moms and dads if it weren't so crowded. In reality, though, they feared entrapment in a shopping frenzy once the moms left the soccer field.

Elk Creek, another small city like Wellington, had always been a rival in school sports activities; it was against the Elk Creek Raiders that Keith had scored the winning touchdown by catching a Hail Mary pass in the end zone—at *their* Homecoming game. The upset dominated the talk of the town for weeks, and Keith figured he wouldn't be the most popular guy on the streets of Elk Creek.

"That was last year," Robby said when the subject came up in the car just before they pulled into the soccer field parking lot. "Nobody will even recognize you anymore."

It *had* been a long time ago, and Keith sincerely hoped that time had properly licked and healed the wounds in Elk Creek. It was all behind them, and Keith didn't want any confrontations; he was here to enjoy a good footy match.

Whether or not it was revenge, the Raiders' crusade was no little challenge for the Wellington Warriors. At half-time, neither team had scored; it appeared obvious that the home squad wasn't about to let a loss on the field ruin their day. They were determined and focused. A win for the Warriors wouldn't come easy.

Long into the second half, after a grueling struggle for control, Kevin realized his chance was near. His teammates were tiring, but so were the Raiders; their reactions were microscopically slower now than at the beginning kick-off. That was something that Kevin had trained himself to observe. He had missed three goal attempts during this game, so far, and now, the Raiders were threatening to score with just two minutes of play remaining. He had to make his move, and fast.

Like a *Patriot* Missile seeking and intercepting a *Scud*, Kevin charged at a low pass, nearly lost control, but regained it to quickly set up his shot.

The Raiders' goalie made a headlong dive to block the kick; when he rose from the field all he had was grass stains on his jersey. The ball was in the net.

Try as they might, the Raiders couldn't change the score, and once again, after the final whistle blew, Kevin was carried off the field on the shoulders of his teammates, some of them exulting in a victory war dance. The Raiders limped their wounded pride back to a sulking crowd of hometown spectators.

Robby imagined a chalkboard in his mind with several hash marks in the 'Win' column, and his hand rising with a stubby chunk of white chalk to add another mark. A few seconds later he exclaimed to Keith and Grant in an excited but subdued shout, not much more than a whisper. "I KNOW WHERE IT IS!" His eyes were like lightning, and although the mid-game excitement of the few Wellington fans on the bleachers and sidelines had diminished to just friendly, happy chatter, Robby was acting as if he were watching Kevin's winning goal all over again.

"PUNKY! BOYS!" Karen Bradley called out and waved. She and the other moms were standing in front of the bleachers, now; the boys still at the top back row. The dads were apparently off to congratulate Kevin and the rest of the team.

"Meet us at Abbey's," Karen said. "We'll pick up Kevin when he gets off the bus... we'll all have supper at Abbey's... about six... okay?"

"Okay, Mom," the three boy choir sang out.

Keith looked at his watch. A few minutes past three. Hour and a half back to Wellington. No doubt, the moms planned to do some power shopping before they left Elk Creek. And by the looks of Robby, it would take that long to bring him out of this crazy stupor he had fallen into.

"Robby!" he said, trying to jerk his buddy back to reality. "What's with you?"

"I know where it is," Robby repeated.

"Where *what* is?"

"I'll tell you in the car."

Now he had both Keith and Grant curious. They hustled him back to the parking lot, stuffed him into the back seat, and Keith climbed in behind the wheel. "I'm driving," he commanded. "You talk."

Once they were out of town, cruising down the open highway back to Wellington, Robby leaned between the front bucket seats so the other two could hear him clearly. That was one of the drawbacks of a top-down convertible—hard to carry on a normal conversation.

He described his vision of a chalkboard and marking on it another win for Kevin's team. It was that vision that had rousted out a recollection from their search of the mineshaft. "I remembered looking at those hundreds of tally marks on the wall near the entrance," he said. "And then I remembered seeing just a *few* marks like them on another wall. At the time it didn't register, and it didn't even seem important. But now I realize that, just like the miners keeping a tally of the ore taken *out* of the mine, Oliver was keeping a tally of the silver bars he was taking *in*."

"So, where were those other marks," Grant said.

"In that first big room we came to... that's where the silver is."

"But we looked pretty thoroughly in there."

"Yeah, well, we missed it somehow," Robby said. "It's got to be there somewhere. Maybe there's a loose rock in the wall that will expose a hidden hole... or something..."

"Well, then," Keith said. "We'll just hafta go back and take another look." Robby had been right about other things—like the 'tiny' stationery store and the hardware store on the wrong side of Main Street, and the alley, and Oliver's path always leading out Flatrock Street. Maybe he was right about the big room, too.

FIFTY-THREE

All of them together at Abbey's required two large tables combined to provide adequate seating for the whole group. Three well-known and well-to-do families dining together meant big tips, so the waitresses scrambled to compete for a share. Even the owner, Russell Abbey, made an appearance to greet them all.

"We're celebrating Kevin's third big win today at Elk Creek," Earl Kraemer proudly informed Russell.

"Yes, I heard," Russell replied. "Someone else who'd been to the game was in just a little while ago." His eyes scanned the group to find Kevin. "Ah, there he is," he said and reached across to shake the star's hand. "Congratulations! You're a legacy in your brother's footsteps."

Kevin beamed and accepted the handshake. "Thank you," he returned.

Grant's face brightened to nearly the color of the red checkered tablecloth when Russell turned to him and winked.

"Good to see you again," he said to Grant, and then he went down the line shaking all the boys' hands. "You guys are all off to college soon, eh?"

"Yes, sir," they all responded politely.

"And Wellington will miss some fine athletes," Russell concluded. "I hope you'll come back to see us when you're in town... and enjoy your meal tonight."

The general conversation around the table was the soccer game at one end among the dads and the boys, and at the other end, the wonderful Christmas ornaments and tablecloths that the moms had acquired at a gift shop in Elk Creek.

Robby participated in the sports talk, but in the back of his mind there churned a very serious and important question he wanted to ask his father. But this wasn't the time or place; it would have to wait for a better, more private opportunity at home.

A couple of hours later, John Gladstone sat in the TV den catching up on the Saturday paper that he had missed earlier that day. *CNN* was on the big screen TV with the volume set low.

"Dad?" Robby said entering the room. "Can we talk? I have something important to ask you."

John dropped the newspaper to his lap. "What do you want to talk about?"

"Dad... if you had a silver ingot, what would you do with it?"

John eyed the boy suspiciously. "What do you mean? Ingot?"

"Like... a seventy-pound ingot... you know... like the ones you can buy over the internet."

John took off his reading glasses and pondered a moment. He had recently received many inquiries regarding gold and silver holdings from his investment clients who were nervous about the current economic stress. "Well... if I had *that* much silver..." He looked at Robby again, this time squinting, puzzled by the question. "Does this have something to do with your little treasure hunt?"

Robby's eyes widened. "You *know* about that?"

"Of course, I know about it. Earl and I had a confidential discussion about it down at the bank one day. That was just before Sheriff Moore dropped in to see me."

"Sheriff Moore?" Robby knew the sheriff had talked to Earl Kraemer, but he wasn't aware of the visit to *his*   father. "What did he—?"

"Earl told me all about your treasure hunt out in the wilderness and about the coins that Kevin found... wanted to know if I had any good advice about rare old coins."

"What did you tell him?"

"That when he found a buyer willing to pay the actual value, I'd find a good, safe investment for Kevin... I'm an expert on investments, not old coins."

"So, are we in trouble with the sheriff?"

"Not yet… Earl and I both agreed that he can't stop you, and if you want to hunt for more old coins out there, there's nothing he can say about it. But we both agreed, too, that you might be wasting your time."

Robby frowned in disappointment.

"Look, Robby," his dad said. "Your grandfather told me all about Silver Spring and its legend… when I was your age. I knew the college kid that worked for him at the newspaper office…"

"You knew Cory Brockway?"

"I met him a few times when Grandpa Vic invited him to our house… nice fellow."

"You do know that he died, don't you?"

"Yes, Grandpa Vic told me."

"So, if you know about Silver Spring and all the stuff that Cory found out, why do you think we're wasting our time?"

"Robby… I found it hard to believe… the legend of a ghost protecting a treasure? Sounded more like a fairy tale to me."

"But Cory must've told you about—"

"Cory was speculating," John interrupted.

"But we've found clues that might prove he wasn't just speculating."

"Clues, clues, and more clues. One will lead you to another, and another… and that's all you're going to find… is more clues."

"But what if Cory *wasn't* just speculating? What if we *really do find something* out there?"

"Then I'll be the *first* to congratulate you."

"Have you ever been out to Silver Spring?"

"No."

"It's a beautiful place."

"I'm sure it is."

"So… what *would* you do with a seventy-pound silver ingot?"

"Put it someplace for safekeeping… hang onto it for a while… that's what I'd do. Silver price is going up… could go through the roof in a couple of years… and that's *my* speculation."

FIFTY-FOUR

Chores, errands, and lawn maintenance kept the boys busy for the next few days. Kevin's footy match on Saturday with the Franklin Tornados and another barbeque—just for the families—to celebrate Grant's eighteenth birthday on Sunday would make another eventful weekend.

Bill and Karen Bradley were preparing for their vacation; in addition to a week in San Francisco, they had scheduled a flight and made reservations for another week in Honolulu. They were leaving on Monday or Tuesday right after the barbeque. That meant Keith would be on his own for two weeks, but not to worry—Mrs. G and Mrs. K would see to it that he got proper nourishment.

Although John Gladstone had tried to convince Robby that hunting for treasure at Silver Spring would be fruitless, that Cory Brockway's journal was merely speculation, Robby couldn't think of anything else; he couldn't abandon the visions of that mineshaft and eleven ingots of pure silver tucked away in some obscure crevice. Keith and Grant had stayed by his side all through the crusade, so far, their assistance indispensable; without them, alone he would have gotten nowhere. But now, he feared they might be losing interest, that their faith in a rewarding finish might be dwindling. By Friday, neither of them had even mentioned another Silver Spring trek. He dared not pressure them; their friendship was far too valuable—with or without the treasure hunt.

The category five tornado attitude of the Franklin team at the opening kick-off in Saturday's soccer match gradually fizzled out to nothing more than a whirlwind that merely kicked up a little dust. Taz Martin's two goals and two more by Kevin clearly set the Wellington Warriors apart from the Franklin Tornados with a 4-1 victory. They had handily weathered another storm.

All the boys wore their Seattle Space Needle T-shirts to the Sunday barbeque as a subtle hint to Bill and Karen Bradley that they expected something similar from Hawaii; they would even settle for San Francisco. The hints were subtly noted.

After some savory shish kebob from Earl's grill, Grant was traditionally honored as the birthday boy; Earl and Judy presented him with a handsome gold watch; the Bradleys gave him a stylish, leather-covered brief case; the package from the Gladstones contained an elegant, gold-plated pen set. All the gifts, of course, were to complement a forthcoming prestigious college lifestyle.

FIFTY-FIVE

"**Hey! Rip Van Winkle!** Your twenty years are up!"

Robby didn't have to open his eyes to know who was in his room, even before Grant called out his greeting. He'd heard both of them on the stairs; Grant and Keith were the only ones who would enter his room without knocking first.

"I'm glad to see you've gotten your fairy tales straight," he said, still a little groggy.

"See? You can't see anything... your eyes are still closed."

"I'm practicing night vision."

"But it's broad daylight."

"That's why my eyes are closed."

"Well, practice time is over. Mrs. G has breakfast waiting, and we're hungry."

Robby opened his eyes and sat up before he was dragged out of bed by his ankles. Slowly, the orientation process developed; it was Monday, Grant was a year older, Mr. and Mrs. B were leaving for their vacation... and there was a treasure to find. That's what had kept him awake so long the night before, thinking about the silver ingots just waiting to be found in that mineshaft.

"I need a shower," he said to the others.

Grant opened the dresser drawer, pulled out clean socks and underwear, and tossed them on the bed beside Robby. "We'll be downstairs in the kitchen... *hungry*," he said, figuring that should be a subtle enough hint for Robby to hustle.

John Gladstone had already left for his office when Robby sat down at the table. Grant and Keith were already working on a stack of pancakes and bacon.

"Are Karen and Bill ready to leave on their vacation?" Phyllis

191

asked Keith.

"Dad's going in this morning to give some last-minute reminders to the people at his office and Mom's doing some last-minute shopping. I think they're planning on taking off this afternoon."

"Well, I'm making lasagna for dinner tonight... if you boys are interested."

Keith's eyes lit up, and then he looked at Grant, then Robby. "When are we going... um... exploring?"

"It's alright," Robby replied. "Dad knows about it, and I'm sure he's told Mom, too."

"Told me about what?" Phyllis asked.

"Our treasure hunt," Robby responded.

"Oh," Phyllis said matter-of-factly. "Of course, I know about that. Where's your next adventure taking you? Deep sea diving in the Gulf of Mexico... or, maybe the mountains of Tibet?"

The boys chuckled.

"We haven't found this one... yet," said Grant.

"And remember, Mrs. G," Keith added. "We're off to college in a month."

Phyllis opened a cupboard door and shuffled some things around. "Yes, and then I won't have anyone to run to the store for me... Robby..."

"What d'ya need now, Mom?"

"A big box of lasagna noodles. Would you—"

"Sure, Mom," they all sang out together.

After they made a dash for the *Hy-Vee* market in the Mustang, the boys stopped to regroup in the back yard. They saw Earl Kraemer through the open fence gate cleaning his grill after Sunday's barbeque.

"Need any help with that, Mr. K?" Keith called to him.

"No, but thanks anyway," Earl replied. "Just about finished."

"So," Robby said. "You guys really want to go back out to Silver Spring?"

"Of course..." Grant replied.

"Why wouldn't we?" Keith added. "We want to help you find your treasure."

"*Our treasure*," Robby corrected him. "Neither of you have said anything for many days... thought you'd lost interest."

"We didn't want to say anything around your dad," Grant said. "And he's been 'round a lot."

"He's known about us going to Silver Spring ever since the sheriff talked to your dad and him..." Robby said. "And I'd be surprised if Sheriff Moore hasn't told *your* dad, too, Keith."

"Sure he did," Keith replied. "He told me the sheriff stopped in to see him one day at his office."

"Seems like there's getting to be too many people who know about this."

"Don't worry 'bout the dads," Keith said. "They're not gonna say anything to anybody."

"So when should we go back out there?"

"This afternoon? After my mom and dad leave."

"I don't want to miss the lasagna tonight."

"Then... how 'bout tomorrow?"

FIFTY-SIX

It was Bon Voyage to the Bradleys about three that afternoon and by five o'clock the boys were hovering around the Gladstone patio door anticipating a bellyful of lasagna. By the next morning they'd had time to plan the Silver Spring trip; time to decide what tools they may need.

"Why don't we open up that other entrance?" Grant questioned. "Sure would make it easier to get in there."

"No," Robby said. "We don't want to make it easy for *someone else*. As it is now, even if someone did go out there, they're not apt to even see the mineshaft. Look how many times we were there and didn't know about it."

They gathered up three small pry bars from their dads' tool collections; all their gear from the previous trip was still in the Jeep.

As if it were just another ordinary day, the boys packed a cooler with Cokes and sandwiches, filled a water jug. Dressed in jeans and hiking boots they piled into the Jeep. Near the edge of town, Grant noticed the green Ford truck parked at the curb, but he didn't get a look at the driver. It was the same truck he'd seen at the soccer match, and he was sure it belonged to someone in the Four Wheeler club. Still not remembering, Grant's curiosity turned him off the highway to go around the block. But when he pulled up to the corner where he had seen the green truck, it was gone. At that point, it didn't seem to matter anymore. Their previous trip to Silver Spring had certainly proved exciting, but it didn't return them home with the rich rewards they had expected. This time, though, things might be different; Robby had discovered the ultimate clue to Oliver's hiding place. Green

194

pickup trucks held little value.

Almost eleven o'clock when they reached their camping spot at the foot of Silver Spring hill, it had been a long time since breakfast, so the salami and cheese sandwiches came out of the cooler. They enjoyed the fare and what had become their favorite place in the world in the shade of oaks and elms. The chickadees welcomed back their visitors, and the ground squirrel periscopes popped up out of the grass for another inquisitive look, quickly converging on the scraps of bread crust the boys tossed to them.

"Let's do it!" Keith said as they gulped down the last swallows of their Cokes and tossed the empty cans in the back of the Jeep. The sun was scorching hot, but they would soon be in the cool depths of the mineshaft.

The rope was once again fastened securely to the trunk of the stout oak tree and Keith, with crow bar and sweatshirt tied around his waist, began the climb down. Then, as before, Robby made his descent, and then Grant followed. At the mouth of the shaft they untied the lantern, water jug, and sweatshirts from their belts, staring into the inky blackness that lay before them.

Keith slipped into his hoodie and switched on the lantern, lighting up the tunnel beyond the pool they would once again have to wade across. He took up the long stick probe from their first mission and started walking slowly toward the pool. Grant and Robby pulled flashlights from their hip pockets and followed Keith.

Nothing had changed; everything appeared just as it had before. Trickling water still echoed from the unknown darkness and the musty smell was pierced every now and then with a wisp of moving air, which they now knew its origin. The spooky darkness, though, now seemed less intimidating when they reached the big cavern. Robby pointed out the chalk marks on the rock wall, right where he remembered they were. They all stared and counted.

Keith leaned the walking stick against a smooth rock wall

surface, and then set the lantern on the ground, aiming it to light a portion of the room to the left of the large pool of water. His giant shadow danced on the wall as he stepped in front of the light to approach the far corner. With his bar, he started tapping and gently prying on the rocks. Grant and Robby each took up positions along the lighted wall to do the same. When they had found no hidden pockets, they moved the lantern and began a thorough probing of the next section.

Nearly two hours of searching everything they could reach had yielded nothing. Keith noticed something curious up higher; he found hand and foot holds to climb while Grant and Robby trained the light on him and watched him inch slowly up the wall like a spider.

"Why are you looking up there?" Robby asked. "Oliver wouldn't have done that."

"Maybe he had a ladder," Keith replied, straining to pull himself up a little more.

But the elevated search found nothing, either.

Keith returned to the floor and the three of them stood huddled together in the middle of the cavern. They were running out of ideas, and it was painfully appearing as though the treasure was lost forever, or someone else had beaten them to it.

"Well, this room was our best shot," Robby said, feeling quite defeated. "I was so sure it would be here... somewhere."

Disappointment was overcoming all three and they were all secretly considering giving up when an eerie scraping noise followed by a thump raised goose bumps in wholesale proportions. Robby swung the light beam toward the noise, only to discover that the walking stick Keith had propped against the wall had fallen. He stared at the stick a few moments. At first, the vision that appeared in his mind was confusing, but then it slowly came into focus, as if some unidentifiable energy was prompting his subconscious thoughts. Just as the vision of the marks on a chalkboard had stirred his awareness of the marks on the mineshaft wall, so was this vision churning a new revelation.

He stepped over to the stick, picked it up and then marched to the edge of the water pool. Thrusting the tip of the stick into the pool, Robby tapped at the bottom like a blind man seeking obstacles with a white cane. Grant and Keith came to his side.

The stick was just long enough to barely reach the far side of the pool. Its tip struck something solid; he traced the outline of the object, detecting the presence of what seemed to be square corners. Grant pointed the light at where Robby had agitated the sediment from the bottom of the pool, but the water was so murky, the light merely reflected off its surface.

Without any hesitation, Robby withdrew the stick, tossed it behind him, and slowly stepped into the knee-deep water, wading to the far side. The water was icy cold, but right then the cold had no impact. He pushed up his sleeves and reached into the water with his hands.

Grant and Keith watched as he felt around the bottom of the pool. Robby grasped one of the brick-like objects with both hands. Even under the water it seemed heavy, but he hoisted it out, carried it to the edge of the pool and plopped it at Keith's feet. He immediately returned to the other side and retrieved another. Setting it next to the first, he climbed out of the cold water.

Glaring up from their feet lay two large, rectangular bricks, each fourteen inches long, four inches wide, and two inches thick, and incredibly shiny.

"I-is this wh-what I think it is?" Keith stuttered.

"Pick it up," Robby said.

Keith bent down and grasped one of the ingots, but after lifting the seventy-pound bar only a few inches, he quickly set it down again, and they all knelt down to admire the find. Rubbing his fingers over the brilliant surface Keith said, "I thought you told us they'd be black..."

"They've been under water," Robby replied. "Not exposed to the air."

"Is there more down there?" Grant asked.

Robby didn't verbally answer; he just looked up at the marks on the wall.

They were mesmerized by the sight; that they had act-ually found the missing silver was utterly amazing; that it was still *there* was nothing short of a miracle.

Then the reality of the moment established its space in time.

"What are you gonna do with 'em?" Keith said.

"We'll take them home," Robby replied. "Dad said we should find a safe place to keep them and hang on to them for a while. They'll be worth a lot more in a couple of years when the silver value goes up."

"How does he know that?"

"It's his business to know stuff like that, and I think we should listen to his advice."

"Okay... but now we hafta get 'em out of here," Grant said. "They're heavy, and it's *not* gonna be easy getting them up that cliff."

"Not so tough," Keith said. "One of us can go up... pull them up with the rope one at a time."

"Sounds like a good plan to me." Robby hoisted one of the bars onto his shoulder. "Grab the other one, Keith... Grant... get our tools and the other stuff... let's go." He was starting to feel the cold from soaking his pants legs in the frigid water.

At the mouth of the tunnel they made a sling with two sweatshirts that would safely hold the weight of the bars and protect them from marring against the rocky cliff wall. As Robby swung away from the mineshaft to begin his ascent to the top, Grant said, "You *will* throw the rope back down to us... right?"

Robby stared back at him. "Yeah, right... like I'm gonna leave you guys stranded here." He laughed.

Keith tied the end of the rope to the sweatshirt sling containing one of the silver ingots and two pry bars, then shouted to Robby. "OKAY, ROBBY... FIRST ONE'S READY... PULL IT UP."

The slack in the rope tightened and then he and Grant

watched the knotted sweatshirt disappear up the side of the cliff. A few minutes later the rope and the sweatshirts came sailing back down. Grant used the walking stick to reach and snag the sling, pulled it back to the mineshaft, and carefully placed the remaining silver ingot, the other pry bar and the lantern in the sling.

"TAKE IT UP, ROBBY," he called out, and the second bar slowly made its journey up to the top.

Grant tied the water jug to his belt, and when the rope dropped down, he swung out and started the climb. "See ya at the top," he said to Keith.

Scanning the area Keith saw nothing else they had left behind; he swung away and pulled himself up the face of the cliff. At the top he reeled in the rope.

FIFTY-SEVEN

Back in the hot sun, Robby took off his jeans, sliced off the wet legs with a knife, and then slipped on the cut-off shorts. Although Grant's jeans were only wet at the cuffs, he did the same. As an act of joyous triumph, they sent the pant legs soaring over the edge of the cliff. Keith just watched and laughed.

The exhilaration of such an accomplishment was nearly overpowering; two months of struggling and risks and secrecy had rewarded them quite handsomely. Now they were in a position to prove to all the doubters—the Moms and Dads, mostly—that their time spent 'exploring' had not been just foolish child's play.

They hoisted the ingots up on a boulder where the sun-rays sparkled on the gleaming silver. The thrill had rendered them totally oblivious to the rest of the world, delirious in their own rapture.

Then everything around them hushed to an abnormal stillness, as if some sinister demon was blackening the sky. Song birds that had seemingly been sharing the boys' merriment with festive melody abruptly stopped singing; all the hum of nature seemed to freeze in the moment. The boys *were* in a ghost town, and they had just imposed on one ghost's cache.

A strange and uncommonly sadistic voice pierced through the joyous celebration. "I see you've found the missing silver."

The boys were jarred from their jubilation. They spun around toward the voice that had sounded from the direction of Tanglewood Lodge... and very close. They had not noticed the man looming toward them. So much for secrecy.

His stealth approach had brought him within twenty feet

undetected until he had spoken. He was a man of about sixty years; rough, leathery skin drooped on his face that hadn't been close to a razor in several days. Faded blue jeans and a dirty white T-shirt with a cigarette pack rolled up in the sleeve hung on his frail-looking frame like limp rags. The thumb of his left hand was hooked in a belt loop and his right hand appeared to be at the small of his back.

He advanced toward the boys slowly and cautiously, his eyes flitting from one to the other to the other, and to the radiant silver ingots.

"Who are you?" Robby asked the stranger.

"Why, don't you recognize me? Rich little banker's boy?" the man sneered. "I'm Mack!" And then he gave a hideous laugh.

"Really..." Grant said. "There *is* no Mack. Who are you?"

"Don't *you* remember me? Little rich boy with the shiny new Jeep? Wanted some driving lessons?"

Grant vaguely remembered a few older Four Wheeler members, but some had not been in the forefront when social or instructional conversations occurred. And this man, perhaps, appeared differently now in shabby clothes and unshaven.

But to Keith, the man struck a familiar note; he said, "Haven't I seen you at Abbey's?"

"Yeah, you have, rich little baker's son," the man snarled.

Keith recalled the stranger across the dining room that had seemed to be staring at their table, and now it appeared evident that it was not just coincidence—he had been paying close attention to their conversation as well.

Robby stepped in front of the silver bars, blocking the man's view of them. His obnoxious behavior was becoming irritating; he was obviously up to no good. "Who *are* you, and what do you want with us?"

"I am Milton Sinclair," the man said, with a sneer that could have crumbled Mount Rushmore.

Robby shuddered. He remembered the name.

Milton lowered his right hand from the small of his back and then leveled an ominous-looking automatic pistol toward the boys. "I'm here to collect my silver."

The boys froze with terror at the sight of the cannon aimed at them. An obnoxious, nosy old man had suddenly become a deadly adversary. A thousand thoughts streaked through Robby's head all at once. This madman would kill them... out here in the wilderness where there was no one to witness... no one to help. Milton Sinclair, the man accused and convicted of shooting and seriously wounding Buck Paxton in 1968... how could he know about the silver?

Milton was nervous, too, perhaps because he knew if he were apprehended again, especially on a charge of assault with a deadly weapon, he would never again know freedom. "I've been watching you boys out here," Milton said. "I knew it was just a matter of time 'til you found the missing bars."

He'd been spying on them! Of course. That explained the weird sensations of being watched, Robby thought. But Sinclair's observable tenseness made the situation worse; he was in a highly volatile state, and that gun looked like it could rip a hole in the side of a battleship. "H-how do you know about the silver?" Robby asked.

"I heard Rich Kid with the shiny new Jeep askin' the four-wheelers about Silver Spring on that trail ride, and then I heard the three of you talkin' 'bout makin' a treasure map at Abbey's... and then I started watchin' you... hardest part was keepin' track of you in all those different cars."

"But how do you know about the silver?" Robby repeated.

"My granddaddy told me 'bout it. Elmer Dickens was my granddaddy... he worked with Oliver Pratt at the smelter... knew that Oliver snuck some silver bars out when he thought no one was looking. But then Oliver got hisself shot dead, and Granddaddy thought he could find the bars that Oliver stole, 'cept he never did... 'n neither did anybody else."

"Did you shoot Buck Paxton in 1968?" Robby asked. "My grandpa Vic always thought you were innocent."

"Well Victor Gladstone was wrong. Yeah, I shot him... but I only meant to scare them... and I spent ten years of my life in prison for that. And I've been lookin' for a way to get my hands on that old journal ever since... heard Cory and Buck talkin' 'bout it when we was still chummin', 'bout the Crane kid seein' Oliver carryin' off the silver bars, but the sheriff never let me look close at it."

"You'll go back to prison again for this," Robby said. "You *know* that, don't you? This silver belongs to us. We found it and you're stealing it."

Milton sneered. He pulled out a cell phone from his jeans pocket. "No," he said. "I'm not going back to prison. How much more is there? Where is it?"

Robby hesitated. He was nervous and scared. A deadly weapon was pointed at his chest. He didn't care, at that moment, about the silver; he wanted to see another sunrise.

Keith abruptly stepped into the line of fire between Sinclair and Robby. "There *is* no more," he said defiantly.

"You're lying," Sinclair barked.

In a low, calm but stern voice, Keith bravely responded. "There is no more. There's the rope... climb down there and look for yourself." He was bluffing; he knew the man was in no physical condition to scale that cliff, and he knew the man was smart enough not to let any of them out of his sight. "And another thing," Keith added. "There's three of us. If there was more, would we only bring out *two* bars? Does that make any sense?"

Milton stared at Keith for a moment, and then briefly glanced at the rope in a pile at the edge of the cliff, the tools and lantern. Quickly he processed the thought: if they had intended to bring out more, their equipment would not be here—it would still be in the mineshaft. Knowing that his only advantage, now, was the gun, he would have to concede to two bars of silver. He pressed a speed-dial button on his phone and put it to his ear. "Ricky," he spoke. "I have the goods... how far are you?"

It was now clear that Milton Sinclair had an accomplice; the circumstances did not look good.

"Half an hour? Good. You know what to do." Sinclair returned the cell phone to his pocket. "Now," he said to the boys. "Let me tell you how this is gonna work."

"You won't get away with this," Robby said, looking around Keith's shoulder.

"SHUT UP!" Milton yelled.

Keith nudged Robby with his elbow. "Mr. Sinclair," he said, addressing the gunman in an attempt to calm him down. "If we let you take the silver bars, will you leave us alone?"

"Oh, I'm taking the silver, little rich boy. You don't deserve to have it… all of you already have anything you want… little rich boys."

"Maybe our fathers are rich," Keith said, "But that doesn't mean *we* are… we're—"

"SHUT UP!" Milton blared. "Now… nobody's gonna get hurt if you do what I say… GOT IT?"

The boys cowered and nodded. There was no hope of any compromise here, and they were looking down the wrong end of the firearm.

"There's a plane waiting for me at the airstrip," Milton began to explain. "Ricky's taking me to South America… oh… and don't come looking for me. South America is a big place and there's lots of bad people there." Milton sneered again, brandishing as much intimidation as he could. "Now, you little rich boys are gonna tote those silver bars to my truck… right up over that hill…" He pointed to the slope behind Tanglewood Lodge. "You see, there's another route to here that you don't know about… shorter… and by the time you get back to your shiny new Jeep and can get back to town, I'll be half-way to the Gulf."

The boys understood, now, how he had been at Silver Spring and they had never detected him.

"Now… first things first… give me your cell phones… don't want you callin' anybody after I leave." He held out his hand, palm up.

Keith was closest to him. He dug in his pocket and pulled out the phone which Sinclair quickly grabbed with a nervous, shaky hand.

"How 'bout you, rich little banker's boy... let's have it." Milton sidestepped so Robby was again in his direct line of sight.

Robby slowly reached for his phone in the front pocket of his jeans and handed it to Sinclair.

Sidestepping again, Milton stood in front of Grant. "Okay... rich kid with the shiny new Jeep... hand it over."

"I-I don't h-have it with me," Grant said meekly.

"I SAID HAND IT OVER!"

Grant fumbled to turn his pockets inside out showing Sinclair they were empty. "I-I left it on my dresser at home."

Sinclair patted Grant's hip pockets. Satisfied that he didn't have a phone, he motioned with the pistol in little waves for them to pick up the silver ingots. "Now, we're gonna go for a little walk," Milton ordered. When Robby and Keith each had one of the bars balanced on his shoulder, Milton pointed them toward the old hotel. They walked single-file with Grant in the lead. At the rear Sinclair called out the directions as they made their way past Tanglewood and up the slope. Over the crest of the hill, a path through the brush dropped down into a narrow valley. Just beyond a small grove of birch trees sat the green Ford pickup.

They had never gone this far beyond Tanglewood; if they had, they might have discovered the trail that Sinclair had mentioned.

"Open the passenger door and put the silver on the floor," Sinclair ordered.

Grant opened the door; Robby and Keith in turn placed their heavy burdens in the truck as directed, backed away with their hands held shoulder high, palms open.

Sinclair tossed the cell phones on the truck seat next to a duffel bag and motioned for Grant to close the door. Grant did as instructed and then quickly joined the others. He stared at the truck; now he associated the green Ford with the man on the trail ride that had been quite unsociable and distant, even to some of the other members.

Milton came at them with his gun hand stretched out in front of him as if aiming.

The boys backed away from him.

"Now, you rich little boys sit right down on the ground," he ordered. "And you stay there for the next ten minutes... you so much as move from that spot and I'll put a slug in every one of you." His intense glare was like a laser. "UNDERSTAND?"

They nodded and sat on the ground.

Sinclair, still keeping the gun trained on them, stepped backwards around the truck, got in the driver's seat, started the engine and drove away. Within seconds the green Ford truck was out of sight, its path hidden by trees and the contour of the hill.

FIFTY-EIGHT

Still in a state of shock, the boys sat there a few moments trying to get their confused thoughts together. Although the incident with Milton Sinclair had lasted a half-hour, at least, it all seemed like a blurry flash.

"What should we do?" Grant asked, his voice still shaky from utter fear.

"Think he's telling the truth about the plane?" Keith said.

"Probably," Robby replied. He, too, was trembling now, thinking about the close encounter with deadly force. "There was a duffel bag in the truck... he had his clothes packed and ready to travel."

"We should try to get to the cops," Grant said.

"Won't matter... he's not apt to stick around long enough for us to get back to town. He's an ex-con, and if we blow the whistle on him... tell the cops that he held us at gunpoint... they'd lock him up and throw away the key."

"What d'ya mean? *If...*" Keith asked.

"Think about it," Robby said. "If we tell *anyone* about this— especially the cops—our secret will be on the nat-ional six o'clock news. Do you want that to happen?"

Keith pondered a long moment. If they reported the incident, their efforts to keep their discovery under wraps to avoid anyone from moving in on the spoils would be to no avail. Questions— too many questions—would be asked, and they would have to reveal the reason why Milton Sinclair had accosted them. "No, of course not," he conceded.

They sat without speaking for several minutes.

Robby finally broke the silence. "Sinclair knew about the

silver because of his grandfather... remember? Elmer Dickens was one of the looters who escaped the gunfight between Clancy Crane and Zach Jr., the bank robber, and apparently he was there then because he was wise to Oliver's thievery, but he didn't know *how much* silver was missing. And Sinclair still doesn't know. When you told him there was no more, I think he might've doubted you, but he couldn't afford the risks of looking when you dared him to climb down and look for himself. That was a good move, Keith." He lightly punched Keith's arm.

"Yeah," Keith said. "I knew he'd be easy to bluff; he couldn't more climb down that rope than my mom could."

"Yeah. And now he's on the run. If he is going to South America, we'll just let him go. If the cops catch up with him, we're ruined."

"But he's got our silver," Grant objected.

"So what! He's gone, and I don't think we have to worry about him coming back... *ever*... and my guess is that he really *is* going to South America where he knows we won't follow him... and he won't *dare* come back here again... risking going back to prison."

A couple more minutes passed in silence. They had sat there, now, for well over the ten minutes that Sinclair had commanded, not because of his mandate—they knew he was on his way to the small Wellington airport, and there was no way he would know if they moved. They had remained because they needed to get rid of their jitters.

"Okay," Keith said. "Are you guys okay?"

Grant and Robby nodded. They had combed out most of the knots in their nerve endings.

"Let's follow his tracks... find out where this trail comes out."

They followed Milton's tracks less than a mile to where the trail ended beside a grove of poplar trees alongside a lonely gravel-surfaced road not much more than one lane wide. They recognized the place; to the right was Wellington; to the left, more hills and valleys, and a bridge that crossed Silver Creek. This was Old Mill Road, appropriately named as it entered

Wellington from the west and curved around the old abandoned feed mill and grain elevator by the railroad tracks. The spot where they stood was only about two miles out of town. The trail they had walked was just barely noticeable, and only because they knew it was there.

"Okay... so now we know a shorter way to Silver Spring," said Keith. "We'd better get back there."

"Think we should go back to the mine and—"

"No," Robby interrupted Grant. "We've made one mistake today... let's not make another."

After determining that there was no feasible way to get the Jeep from their camp to the new trail, they headed for Wellington by their usual route, their first destination being the airfield. If Milton Sinclair really did leave via the waiting plane, then his truck would be there, and maybe there was an outside chance Robby's and Keith's cell phones would be there, too.

Wellington's airport consisted of numerous private and commercial hangers and a single paved runway long enough to accommodate some commercial planes. But the town was not large enough to attract any airlines, so there was no terminal, no control tower, and no full-time attendants. Sometimes there was so little activity, the place seemed deserted. Today was one of those days.

It would have been difficult to justify their reason for being there; they had no plane; none of their family or friends had planes. Although the airfield was a municipal holding and was quite public, the boys felt like they were treading on someone's private space, like thieves looking for open garage doors. As they drove slowly among the hangers, they spotted Milton's green truck parked in an alley between two buildings. The license plates had been stripped off. It seemed apparent that Milton Sinclair didn't intend to return to his truck anytime soon.

The entire place was as lifeless as a cemetery. Not a single hanger door was open, and not a single person stirred anywhere—no one to ask if they had seen the driver of the green truck leave in an airplane, and no one to question them about why they were snooping in the green truck. But the cell phones weren't there; Milton might have taken them with him, or he might have tossed them out along the road somewhere. No worry. They'd have the phones deactivated right away.

One thing could be certain: Milton Sinclair was gone for good.

It was nearly five-thirty. Supper would soon be ready. During the ride across town, it was decided that absolute secrecy regarding the day's events should remain steadfast. There was no need to report the incident with Milton Sinclair; fortunately, they had not been physically harmed—other than the scare of a lifetime, but they were still young and resilient, and they could eventually recover from that. Even though Milton Sinclair was a criminal, a scoundrel, a thief, his exile to South America was, perhaps, the best ending for him. As far as they were concerned, Milton Sinclair didn't exist.

To nearly everyone in Wellington, Silver Spring was nothing more than a dust-covered mystery. And it would stay that way. The legend of Mack would live on. It had to. For now, he was the only sentinel protecting their secret.

After supper, Robby joined his father in the TV den.

"How'd the treasure hunt go today," John asked from behind his newspaper.

"Um... Dad... I've been meaning to talk to you about that..."

EPILOG:
LEGENDS ARE FOREVER

Robby Gladstone passed the bar after seven long years at Harvard. By that time, Grant Kraemer had operated a computer consulting firm for two and a half years after his four years at Berkley, and Keith Bradley was busy turning out architectural plans after studying civil engineering at the University of Colorado.

But they had stayed in close contact throughout their college years, and their dreams of owning Silver Spring had actually sprouted to reality during that time. Partnering a real estate agency seemed their best option; they could each continue to practice their professions, and still pursue—together—their passionate desire to see Silver Spring live.

Renovating a 120-year-old building that had been abandoned 110 of those years was no small task. But large tasks were nothing new to the Bradley, Gladstone & Kraemer Agency. Their love and affection for Tanglewood Lodge and the utopian countryside where it stood was no small matter, either, and after a six-month-long struggle to acquire the five hundred acres where the historic hotel and its city had once thrived, rejuvenation of the old edifice began. Their long-term plan was to resurrect a large portion of Silver Spring, and now, three years after the project had begun, six buildings on original Main Street foundations are complete, reflecting the stylish flare of the silver mining town as it had appeared in 1890. How they had financed their project remains a mystery; they had never disclosed to anyone their windfall discovery at the Silver Spring mine, and no one can be certain of the contents of the vault in the Tanglewood cellar.

Tanglewood Lodge, originally built as a hotel, no longer functions in that capacity. Although the outward appearance was restored nearly to its original, only the front entrance, staircase, and barroom portion of the interior retained its 1890s decor, replete with upright piano, pot-belly stove, and authentic antique wooden furniture. The rest, though, was fashioned in a more modern, more practical design. The rear part of the lower floor houses several spacious offices for the "Boys" where clients and business agendas are top priority. Three luxury apartments occupy the upper level where Robin Gladstone and his fiancée, Mr. and Mrs. Grant Kraemer, and bachelor Keith Bradley reside quite comfortably on part-time schedules.

In time, Silver Spring will once again be alive, not as a modern, noisy commercial center, but rather, as a functioning, dynamic attraction, a long-lost Wild West mining town. Its brick and cobblestone streets, its board sidewalks, its vintage shops and stores with the names they once bore in the Nineteenth Century stenciled across their false fronts welcome visitors from far and wide.

Legends do not often die easily. This one certainly didn't. But instead of being feared as it had been in the past, the ghosts of Silver Spring are now the main attraction, accepted by the people of Wellington, and craved by tourists seeking a brush with the past. But that's another story.

A town that was once relegated to obscurity by superstition and legend has been resurrected, only because three adventurous young men—Robby Gladstone, Grant Kraemer, and Keith Bradley—had dared to venture *across the dead line*.

And they are right where they wanted to be.

ABOUT THE AUTHOR

Born into a farm family in the late 1940s, J.L. Fredrick lived his youth in rural Western Wisconsin, a modest but comfortable life not far from the Mississippi River. His father was a farmer, and his mother, an elementary school teacher. He attended a one-room country school for his first seven years of education.

Wisconsin has been home all his life, with exception of a few years in Minnesota and Florida. After college in La Crosse, Wisconsin and a stint with Uncle Sam during the Viet Nam era, the next few years were unsettled as he explored and experimented with life's options. He entered into the transportation industry in 1975, where he remained until retirement in 2012.

Since 2001 he has eleven published novels to his credit, and one non-fiction history volume, *Rivers, Roads, & Rails.* He was a featured author during Grand Excursion 2004.

J.L. Fredrick currently resides at Poynette, Wisconsin.

www.ingramcontent.com/pod-product-compliance
Lightning Source LLC
Chambersburg PA
CBHW051509260626
47162CB00008B/2883